Ghost Traps

Ghost Traps

Stories by Robert H. Abel

The University of Georgia Press

Athens and London

© 1991 by Robert H. Abel
Published by the University of Georgia Press
Athens, Georgia 30602
All rights reserved

Set in Linotron 10 on 14 Trump Mediaeval
The paper in this book meets the guidelines for
permanence and durability of the Committee on
Production Guidelines for Book Longevity of the Council
on Library Resources.

Printed in the United States of America

95 94 93 92 91   5 4 3 2 1

Library of Congress Cataloging in Publication Data

Abel, Robert H., date.
    Ghost Traps : stories / by Robert H. Abel.
        p.   cm.
    Contents: Appetizer—A good investment—
    Commander of the buffaloes—My Kline syndrome—
    Lawless in New York—New line—The connoisseur—
    One up—Buck and Tracey go walking—The deaths of
    strangers—A sweepstakes story—Ghost traps.
    ISBN 0-8203-1252-5 (alk. paper)
        I. Title.
    PS3551.B337P55   1991
813'.54—dc20   90-34243
                                              CIP

British Library Cataloging in Publication Data available

To Joyce

Contents

Ghost Traps

Appetizer

I'm fishing this beautiful stream in Alaska, catching salmon, char and steelhead, when this bear lumbers out of the woods and down to the stream bank. He fixes me with this half-amused, half-curious look which says: You are meat.

The bear's eyes are brown and his shiny golden fur is standing up in spikes, which shows me he has been fishing, too, perhaps where the stream curves behind the peninsula of woods he has just trudged through. He's not making any sound I can hear over the rumble of the water in the softball-sized rocks, but his presence is very loud.

I say "his" presence because temporarily I am not interested in or able to assess the creature's sex. I am looking at a head that is bigger around than my steering wheel, a pair of paws awash in river bubbles that could cover half my windshield. I am glad that I am wearing polarized fishing glasses so the bear cannot see the little teardrops of fear that have crept into the corner of my eyes. To assure him/her I am not the least bit intimidated, I make another cast.

Immediately I tie into a fat Chinook. The splashing of the fish in the stream engages the bear's attention, but he/she registers this for the moment only by shifting his/her glance. I play the fish smartly and when it comes gliding in, tired, pink-sided, glittering and astonished, I pluck it out of the water by inserting a finger in its gill—something I normally wouldn't do in order not to injure the fish before I set it free, and I do exactly what you would do in the same situation—throw it to the bear.

The bear's eyes widen and she—for I can see now past her huge shoulder and powerful haunches that she is a she—turns and pounces on the fish with such speed and nimbleness that I am numbed. There is no chance in hell that I, in my insulated waders, am going to outrun her, dodge her blows, escape her jaws. While she is occupied devouring the fish—I can hear her teeth clacking together—I do what you or anyone else would do and cast again.

God answers my muttered prayer and I am blessed with the strike of another fat salmon, like the others on its way to spawning grounds upstream. I would like this fish to survive and release its eggs or sperm to perpetuate the salmon kingdom, but Ms. Bear has just licked her whiskers clean and has now moved knee-deep into the water and, to my consternation, leans against me rather like a large and friendly dog, although her ears are at the level of my shoulder and her back is broader than that of any horse I have ever seen. Ms. Bear is intensely interested in the progress of the salmon toward us, and her head twists and twitches as the fish circles, darts, takes line away, shakes head, rolls over, leaps.

With a bear at your side, it is not the simplest thing to play a fish properly, but the presence of this huge animal, and especially her long snout, thick as my thigh, wonderfully concentrates the mind. She smells like the forest floor, like crushed moss and damp leaves, and she is as warm as a radiator back in my Massachusetts home, the thought of which floods me with a terrible nostalgia. Now I debate whether I should just drift the salmon in under the bear's nose and let her take it that way, but I'm afraid she will break off my fly and leader and right now that fly—a Doctor Wilson number eight—is saving my life. So, with much anxiety, I pretend to take charge and bring the fish in on the side away from the bear, gill and quickly unhook it, turn away from the bear and toss the fish behind me to the bank.

The bear wheels and clambers upon it at once, leaving a vortex of water pouring into the vacuum of the space she has left, which almost topples me. As her teeth snack away, I quickly and furtively regard my poor Doctor Wilson, which is fish-mauled now, bedraggled, almost unrecognizable. But the present emergency compels me to zing it out once again. I walk a few paces downstream, hoping the bear will remember an appointment or become distracted and I can sneak away.

But a few seconds later she is leaning against me again, raptly watching the stream for any sign of a salmon splash. My luck holds; another fish smacks the withered Wilson, flings sunlight and water in silver jets as it dances its last dance. I implore the salmon's forgiveness: something I had once read revealed that this is the way of all primitive hunters, to take the life reluctantly and to pray for the victim's return. I think my prayer is as urgent as that of any Mashpee or Yoruban, or Tlingit or early Celt, for I not only want the salmon to thrive forever, I want a superabundance of them now, right now, to save my neck. I have an idea this hungry bear, bereft of fish, would waste little time in conducting any prayer ceremonies before she turned me into the main course my salmon were just the appetizer for. When I take up this fish, the bear practically rips it from my hand, and the sight of those teeth so close, and the truly persuasive power of those muscled, pink-rimmed jaws, cause a wave of fear in me so great that I nearly faint.

My vertigo subsides as Ms. Bear munches and destroys the salmon with hearty shakes of her head and I sneak a few more paces downstream, rapidly also with trembling fingers tie on a new Doctor Wilson, observing the utmost care (as you would, too) in making my knots. I cast and stride downstream, wishing I could just plunge into the crystalline water and bowl away like a log. My hope and plan is to wade my way back to the narrow trail a few hundred yards ahead and, when Ms. Bear loses interest or is somehow distracted, make a heroic dash for my camper. I think of the thermos of hot coffee on the front seat, the six-pack of beer in the cooler, the thin rubber mattress with the blue sleeping bag adorning it, warm wool socks in a bag hanging from a window crank, and almost burst into tears, these simple things, given the presence of Ms. Hungry Bear, seem so miraculous, so emblematic of the life I love to live. I promise the gods—American, Indian, African, Oriental—that if I survive I will never complain again, not even if my teenage children leave the caps off the toothpaste tubes or their bicycles in the driveway at home.

"Oh, home," I think, and cast again.

Ms. Bear rejoins me. You may or may not believe me, and perhaps after all it was only my imagination worked up by terror, but two things happened which gave me a particle of hope. The first was that Ms. Bear actually belched—quite noisily and unapologetically, too, like a rude uncle at a Christmas dinner. She showed no signs of having committed any impropriety, and yet it was clear to me that a belching bear is probably also a bear with a pretty-full belly. A few more salmon and perhaps Ms. Bear would wander off in search of a berry dessert.

Now the second thing she did, or that I imagined she did, was to begin—well, not *speaking* to me exactly, but *communicating* somehow. I know it sounds foolish, but if you were in my shoes—my waders, to be more precise—you might have learned bear talk pretty quickly, too. It's not as if the bear were speaking to me in complete sentences and English words such as "Get me another fish, pal, or you're on the menu," but in a much more indirect and subtle way, almost in the way a stream talks through its bubbling and burbling and rattling of rocks and gurgling along.

Believe me, I listened intently, more with my mind than with my ears, as if the bear were telepathizing, and—I know you're not going to believe this, but it's true, I am normally not what you would call an egomaniac with an inflated self-esteem such that I imagine that every bear which walks out of the woods falls in love with me—but I really did truly believe now that this Ms. Bear was expressing feelings of, well, *affection*. Really, I think she kinda liked me. True or not, the feeling made me less afraid. In fact, and I don't mean this in any erotic or perverse kind of way, but I had to admit, once my fear had passed, my feelings were kinda mutual. Like you might feel for an old pal of a dog. Or a favorite horse. I only wish she weren't such a big eater. I only wish she were not a carnivore, and I, carne.

Now she nudges me with her nose.

"All right, all right," I say. "I'm doing the best I can."

Cast in the glide behind that big boulder, the bear telepathizes me. *There's a couple of whoppers in there.*

I do as I'm told and wham! the bear is right! Instantly I'm tied into a granddaddy Chinook, a really burly fellow who has no intention of lying down on anybody's platter beneath a blanket of lemon slices and scallion shoots, let alone make his last wiggle down a bear's gullet. Even the bear is excited and begins shifting weight from paw to paw, a little motion for her that nevertheless has big consequences for me as her body slams against my hip, then slams again.

Partly because I don't want to lose the fish, but partly also because I want to use the fish as an excuse to move closer to my getaway trail, I stumble downstream. This fish has my rod bent into an upside-down *U* and I'm hoping my quick-tied knots are also strong enough to take this salmon's lurching and his intelligent, broadside swinging into the river current —a very smart fish! Ordinarily I might take a long time with a fish like this, baby it in, but now I'm putting on as much pressure as I dare. When the salmon flips into a little side pool, the bear takes matters into her own hands, clambers over the rocks, pounces, nabs the salmon smartly behind the head and lumbers immediately to the bank. My leader snaps at once and while Ms. Bear attends to the destruction of the fish, I tie on another fly and make some shambling headway downstream. Yes, I worry about the hook still in the fish, but only because I do not want this bear to be irritated by anything. I want her to be replete and smug and doze off in the sun. I try to telepathize as much. Please, Bear, sleep.

Inevitably, the fishing slows down, but Ms. Bear does not seem to mind. Again she belches. Myself, I am getting quite a headache and know that I am fighting exhaustion. On a normal morning of humping along in waders over these slippery softball-sized rocks, I would be tired in any case. The added emergency is foreclosing on my energy reserves. I even find myself getting a little angry, frustrated at least, and I marvel at the bear's persistence, her inexhaustible doggedness. And appetite. I catch fish, I toss them to her. At supermarket prices, I calculate she has eaten about six hundred dollars worth of fish. The calculating gives me something to think about besides my fear.

At last I am immediately across from the opening to the trail which twines back through the woods to where my camper rests in the dapple shade of mighty pines. Still, five hundred yards separate me from this imagined haven. I entertain the notion perhaps someone else will come along and frighten the bear away, maybe someone with a dog or a gun, but I have already spent many days here without seeing another soul, and in fact have chosen to return here for that very reason. I have told myself for many years that I really do love nature, love being among the animals, am restored by wilderness adventure. Considering that right now I would like nothing better than to be nestled beside my wife in front of a blazing fire, this seems to be a sentiment in need of some revision.

Now, as if in answer to my speculations, the bear turns beside me, her rump pushing me into water deeper than I want to be in, where my footing is shaky, and she stares into the woods, ears forward. She has heard something I cannot hear, or smelled something I cannot smell, and while I labor back to shallower water and surer footing, I hope some backpackers or some bear-poaching Indians are about to appear and send Ms. Bear a-galloping away. Automatically, I continue casting, but I also cannot help glancing over my shoulder in hopes of seeing what Ms. Bear sees. And in a moment I do.

It is another bear.

Unconsciously, I release a low moan, but my voice is lost in the guttural warning of Ms. Bear to the trespasser. The new arrival answers with a defiant cough. He—I believe it is a he—can afford to be defiant because he is half again as large as my companion. His fur seems longer and coarser, and though its substance is as golden as that of the bear beside me, the tips are black and this dark surface ripples and undulates over his massive frame. His nostrils are flared and he is staring with profound concentration at me.

Now I am truly confused and afraid. Would it be better to catch another salmon or not? I surely cannot provide for two of these beasts and in any case Mister Bear does not seem the type to be distracted by or made friendly by any measly salmon tribute. His whole bearing—pardon the expression— tells me my intrusion into this bear world is a personal affront to his bear honor. Only Ms. Bear stands between us and, after all, whose side is she really on? By bear standards, I am sure a rather regal and handsome fellow has made his appearance. Why should the fur-covered heart of furry Ms. Bear go out to me? How much love can a few hundred dollars worth of salmon buy? Most likely, this couple even have a history, know and have known each other from other seasons even though for the moment they prefer to pretend to regard each other as total strangers.

How disturbed I am is well illustrated by my next course of action. It is completely irrational, and I cannot account for it, or why it saved me—if indeed it did. I cranked in my line and lay my rod across some rocks, then began the arduous process of pulling myself out of my waders while trying to balance myself on those awkward rocks in that fast water. I tipped and swayed as I tugged at my boots, pushed my waders down, my arms in the foaming, frigid water, then the waders also filling, making it even more difficult to pull my feet free.

I emerged like a nymph from a cocoon, wet and trembling. The bears regarded me with clear stupefaction, as if one of them had casually stepped out of his or her fur. I drained what water I could from the waders, then dropped my fly rod into them, and held them before me. The damned rocks were brutal on my feet, but I marched toward the trail opening, lifting and dropping first one, then the other leg of my waders as if I were operating a giant puppet. The water still in the waders gave each footfall an impressive authority, and I was half thinking that, well, if the big one attacks, maybe he'll be fooled into chomping the waders first and I'll at least now be able to run. I did not relish the idea of pounding down the trail in my nearly bare feet, but it was a damn sight better way to argue with the bear than being sucked from my waders like a snail from its shell. Would you have done differently?

Who knows what the bears thought, but I tried to make

myself look as much as possible like a camel or some other extreme and inedible form of four-footedness as I plodded along the trail. The bears looked at each other, then at me as I clomped by, the water in the waders making an odd gurgling sound, and me making an odd sound, too, on remembering just then how the Indians would, staring death in the eye, sing their death song. Having no such melody prepared, and never having been anything but a bathtub singer, I chanted forth the only song I ever committed to memory: "Jingle Bells."

Yes, "Jingle Bells," I sang, "jingle all the way," and I lifted first one, then the other wader leg and dropped it stomping down. "Oh what fun it is to ride in a one-horse open sleigh-ay!"

The exercise was to prove to me just how complicated and various is the nature of the bear. The male reared up, blotting out the sun, bellowed, then twisted on his haunches and crashed off into the woods. The female, head cocked in curiosity, followed at a slight distance, within what still might be called striking distance whether I was out of my waders or not. Truly, I did not appreciate her persistence. Hauling the waders half full of water before me was trying work and the superfluous thought struck me: suppose someone sees me now, plumping along like this, singing "Jingle Bells," a bear in attendance? Vanity, obviously, never sleeps. But as long as the bear kept her distance I saw no reason to change my *modus operandi.*

When I came within about one hundred feet of my camper, its white cap gleaming like a remnant of spring snow and beckoning me, I risked everything, dropped the waders and sped for the cab. The bear broke into a trot, too, I was sure, because although I couldn't see her, had my sights locked on the gleaming handle to the pickup door, I sure enough could hear those big feet slapping the ground behind me in a heavy rhythm, a terrible and elemental beat that sang to me of my own frailty, fragile bones and tender flesh. I plunged on like a madman, grabbed the camper door and hurled myself in.

I lay on the seat panting, curled like a child, shuddered when the bear slammed against the pickup's side. The bear pressed her nose to the window, then curiously, unceremoniously licked the glass with her tongue. I know (and you know) she could have shattered the glass with a single blow, and I tried to imagine what I should do if indeed she resorted to this simple expedient. Fisherman that I am, I had nothing in the cab of the truck to defend myself with except a tire iron, and that not readily accessible behind the seat I was cowering on. My best defense, obviously, was to start the pickup and drive away.

Just as I sat up to the steering wheel and inserted the key, however, Ms. Bear slammed her big paws onto the hood and hoisted herself aboard. The pickup shuddered with the weight of her, and suddenly the windshield was full of her golden fur. I beeped the horn loud and long numerous times, but this had about the same effect as my singing, only caused her to shake her huge head, which vibrated the truck terribly. She stomped around on the hood and then lay down, back against the windshield, which now appeared to have been covered by a huge shag rug.

Could I believe my eyes?

No, I could not believe my eyes. My truck was being smothered in bear. In a moment I also could not believe my ears— Ms. Bear had decided the camper hood was the perfect place for a nap, and she was *snoring*, snoring profoundly, her body twitching like a cat's. Finally, she had responded to my advice and desires, but at the most inappropriate time. I was trapped. Blinded by bear body!

My exhaustion had been doubled by my sprint for the camper, and now that I was not in such a desperate panic, I felt the cold of the water that had soaked my clothes and I began to tremble. It also crossed my mind that perhaps Mister Bear was still in the vicinity, and if Ms. Bear was not smart enough, or cruel enough, to smash my window to get at me, he just might be.

Therefore, I started the engine—which disturbed Ms. Bear not a whit—and rolled down the window enough to stick my head out and see down the rocky, limb-strewn trail. I figured a few jolts in those ruts and Ms. Bear would be off like a shot.

This proved a smug assumption. Ms. Bear did indeed awaken and bestir herself to a sitting position, a bit like an overgrown hood ornament, but quickly grew quite adept at balancing herself against the lurching and jolting of my truck, which, in fact, she seemed to enjoy. Just my luck, I growled, to find the first bear in Alaska who wanted a ride into town. I tried some quick braking and sharp turn maneuvers I thought might send her tumbling off, but her bulk was so massive, her paws so artfully spread, that she was just too stable an entity. She wanted a ride and there was nothing I could do about it.

When I came out of the woods to the gravel road known locally as the Dawson Artery, I had an inspiration. I didn't drive so fast that if Ms. Bear decided to clamber down she would be hurt, but I did head for the main road which led to Buckville and the Buckville Cannery. Ms. Bear swayed happily along the whole ten miles to that intersection and seemed not to bat an eye when first one big logging truck, then another plummeted by. I pulled out onto the highway, and for the safety of both of us—those logging trucks have dubious brakes and their drivers get paid by the trip—I had to accelerate considerably.

I couldn't see much of Ms. Bear except her back and rump as I had to concentrate on the road, some of which is pretty curvy in that coastal area, shadowed also by the giant pines.

But from the attitude expressed by her posture, I'd say she was having a whale, or should I say a salmon of a time. I saw a few cars and pickups veering out of the oncoming lane onto the shoulder as we swept by, but I didn't have time, really, to appreciate the astonishment of their drivers. In this way, my head out the window, Ms. Bear perched on the hood, I drove to the Buckville Cannery and turned into the long driveway.

Ms. Bear knew right away something good was ahead for she rose on all fours now and stuck her nose straight out like a bird dog on a pheasant. Her legs quivered with nervous anticipation as we approached, and as soon as I came out of the trees into the parking area, she went over the front of the camper like someone plunging into a pool.

Don't tell me you would have done any differently. I stopped right there and watched Ms. Bear march down between the rows of cars and right up the truck ramp into the cannery itself. She was not the least bit intimidated by all the noise of the machines and the grinders and stampers in there, or the shouting of the workers.

Now the Buckville Cannery isn't that big—I imagine about two dozen people work there on any given day—and since it is so remote, has no hurricane fence around it, and no security guard. After all, what's anybody going to steal out of there besides a few cases of canned salmon or some bags of frozen fish parts that will soon become some company's cat food? The main building is up on a little hill and conveyors run down from there to the docks where the salmon boats pull in—the sea is another half mile away—and unload their catch.

I would say that in about three minutes after Ms. Bear walked into the cannery, twenty of the twenty-four workers were climbing out down the conveyors, dropping from open windows, or charging out the doors. The other four just hadn't got wind of the event yet, but in a little while they came bounding out, too, one fellow pulling up his trousers as he ran. They all assembled on the semicircular drive before the main office and had a union meeting of some vigor.

Myself, I was too tired to participate, and in any case did not want to be held liable for the disturbance at the Buckville Cannery, and so I made a U-turn and drove on into Buckville itself where I took a room above the Buckville Tavern and had a hot shower and a really nice nap. That night in the Tap and Lounge I got to hear many an excited story about the she-bear who freeloaded at the cannery for a couple of hours before she was driven off by blowing, ironically enough, the lunch whistle loud and long. I didn't think it was the right time or place to testify to my part in that historical event, and for once kept my mouth shut. You don't like trouble any more than I do, and I'm sure you would have done about the same.

A Good Investment

"What is it, darling?" Victor spoke mildly, even though he had asked his wife not to disturb him when he was in his study, and had sometimes responded to her intrusions with impatience and sarcasm. But tonight he was not really working very hard. He closed the portfolio with an air of bored satisfaction.

Janice had an abstracted look on her face, as if she had just forgotten the reason for this violation of Victor's Law. She did not speak for so long that Victor felt it necessary to prod her along. "Is it something important?"

"I'm sorry," she said. "I thought it was. I suppose I'm being silly. I was sitting there, and I was suddenly afraid."

"Afraid?" Victor said, a little disapprovingly, for he detected a slight slur in her speech that suggested she had been drinking again. She was growing entirely too lazy and in consequence was losing both mental sharpness, which had always been considerable—one of the reasons he married her—and her formerly fine figure. In her Victor thought he was seeing in the flesh an example of what was meant by "going soft," and he didn't like it at all.

"I thought I saw a face," Janice said, and then laughed unpleasantly. "Outside, at the window."

Victor grew serious, capped his pen and stood up. "I'll have a look," he said.

"I'm not sure," Janice said, folding her hands on her stomach.

"Well, we'll make sure."

"What should I do?"

"Do?" Victor squeezed her shoulder as he passed by. "Stay by the telephone. If I shout, call the police."

He stopped at the hall closet, rummaged for a flashlight, and found the one he carried with him on the boat, one that would float if you dropped it overboard. He wished now he had one of those which were long and silver, for that kind could also be used in a pinch as a club. His son Robert was always hounding him to buy a pistol, but Victor had avoided doing that, he said, because he did not believe in guns and the country was too violent a place anyway. But the real reason was that he did not trust himself enough to own a gun, and there were plenty of people he had fantasied using one on, including his own wife. But as he went through the front door now, he thought, yes, a pistol would be a comfort.

He flicked on the light, looked quickly behind the shrubs along the front of the house, then moved to the left side, flashed along the walls and into the shrubbery, then doubled back across the front in case a prowler had been there and was trying to elude his search by circling the house. Victor didn't really want an encounter with any prowler, but could not stop himself from making this artful little move, for more than he feared running into a thug he feared being thought stupid by one. Most likely, though, the prowler was all in Janice's mind. She had been damned moody lately, scared silly of every little thing.

Victor moved quickly up the driveway past the garage and sprayed the light back and forth over the rear of the house and the back lawn. The swimming pool glimmered blue and green as he spanned it with the light. He checked the side door to the garage—it was locked—and flashed the light through the window. Nothing was awry, and in fact the interior of his car seemed inviting and peaceful, doubly insulated from the world.

The night itself was calm, a bit humid, but very pleasant. Of course, that wouldn't matter to murderers. A nice night for a murder, that's all they would think, Victor surmised.

Light fanned across the lawn now as Janice opened the back door and peered into the darkness.

"Victor?"

"I'm right here."

"I called the police. They said others had complained, too. A car's been sent. Maybe you should come in."

"I didn't find anything . . ."

"Victor!" Janice shouted, pointing up, and Victor turned and aimed the light where she had indicated, absurdly high. The beam swept to the gable over the garage doors, over a pair of black shoes, then two bare, dangling legs, settled on a little, fat man, squinting, chewing, dressed only in cotton briefs. The man's flesh seemed too pale, garishly white in the flashlight beam. He chewed slowly, as if only mildly perturbed at being discovered, or like some animal just prodded from hibernation.

"Victor! Get in here!"

"Yeah, yeah," Victor said. "Call the police. Tell 'em what we've got." In Victor's eyes, the man had no intention of moving. In fact, he seemed in a little bit of a predicament, a cat up a tree, and in any case was too far away to be immediately dangerous. He clearly wasn't armed.

"*In* here!" Janice's voice cracked.

Victor backed to the rear stoop, keeping the man fixed in the beam of light. Janice snapped on the spotlights over the garage and the whole yard was illuminated, the flashlight superfluous. Victor kept the beam on the man's face, however, sure that it kept him disoriented and unable to see well. Victor had been on the other side of flashlights himself, blinded by that insistent, irritating brilliance. The house was only a few feet behind now and he felt safe enough, if just a little uneasy. He could hear Janice reporting to the police, and the words seemed almost comic: ". . . on the roof of our garage, and he's naked."

Victor snapped off the flashlight and the pale white figure dissolved suddenly into a dark, pathetic lump. Victor continued to observe the man, wondering how such a creature, so doughy and flaccid, could have grappled his way to such a height.

"Hey, fella," he called out. "What are you doing up there anyway?"

"Just leave him alone and get in here," Janice, behind him again, insisted. "*Please*, Victor."

"Hey, fella," Victor pressed on. "You want something? Water?"

"Don't you go near him!" Janice said.

Before she had even finished her plea, Victor was aware of the beginning of something, like the *meow* of a cat, a high-pitched, grating sound that, in the wake of Janice's voice, emerged suddenly and clearly as a wail of grief. The man on the roof was attempting a song of sorts, and he leaned back with his hands in his lap and raised his voice in a cry of such sirenlike sadness that Victor trembled, as if chilled.

"Oh!" Janice whispered. "Oh God, Victor."

"Are you hurt?" Victor called. "Do you need medicine or something like that?"

The man's only reply was to wail all the more loudly and more plaintively still.

Victor was about to call out another question when car lights splashed the front of the garage and a powerful beam fell on the man like a net, so that he seemed momentarily to leap out of the darkness, or to catch fire. He only turned his head away from the glare and continued his strange wail. Shadows of the policemen danced across the garage, growing smaller and sharper as the men came forward. When they passed the corner of the house, they seemed very small indeed.

"You folks all right?" The officer who spoke was shorter than his companion, and also black and extremely broad-shouldered. His holster rode so low on his hip that it seemed it could not possibly stay in place. The other officer was white, paunchy, with a deeply creased face. He looked very tired.

"We're fine," Victor said. "He hasn't done anything but sit up there."

"He looked in our windows first," Janice corrected him. She stepped out of the house now and took hold of Victor's arm.

"All right, Jackie," the black officer called. "We'll get you down from there and you can come with us."

"How'd you get up there?" the other officer asked. "Hey? You hear me?"

The man answered with a wail.

"I left some ladders around back of the garage," Victor said. "He might've used those."

The black officer looked Victor's way and said, "Oh, Jackie likes to climb all right. He doesn't often need a ladder."

"You know him well?" Victor asked.

"We know him well," the white cop said wearily. "He's off his turf tonight, though. New neighborhood."

"Jackie, you going to make us come up there or what?" The black cop adjusted his gear, then folded his arms across his chest.

"You come up. Sure." The clarity of the man's voice stunned Victor. He realized he had been thinking of him as an animal of some kind, an ape or a bull, or a big dog. He hadn't expected *speech.*

"We don't want to come up," the white cop growled. "It'd be better if you just came down."

"Not better," Jackie said.

"Aren't you getting cold?" the black cop asked. "We'll turn the heater on for you, in the car."

"Not better," Jackie said.

"Come on, Jackie," the white cop pled. "Don't make us come up there tonight. We'll get mad if we have to climb up there for you."

Out of the darkness the man's voice drifted down again. "Die," it commanded.

The cops looked at each other, and then the black one turned to Victor. "You mind if we use your ladders?"

"Of course not," Victor said. "Just don't sue me if you fall."

"I hate this," the white cop complained loudly. "I'd just as soon shoot the sonabitch. Or let the dogcatcher handle it. This is ridiculous!"

"Jackie?" the black cop said. "Roy's getting madder by the minute. Maybe you'd just better come down."

"You're damn right I'm mad!" Roy said. "I got to risk my neck for a stupid jerk like you? I'm tired of it."

"O.K., Roy, simmer down," the black cop said, loud enough for everyone to hear.

"The hell I will," Roy said. "Do I look like a baby-sitter? You think we don't have more important things to do? Who the hell does this guy think he is? Wastin' our time!"

"Roy's really mad now," the black cop called up to the man. "Maybe you'd better just come down right now. I can't calm him down. You want me to help you?"

"Yes," the man said. The lump on the garage roof seemed to shrivel, and then rolled over, away from the lights.

"You think he'll really come down now?" Roy asked his partner.

"You get on that side, I'll stay on this," the black cop said. "He might slide down, then run for it."

"I don't feel like climbin'," Roy said, "and I don't feel like runnin', either."

They fanned out, the black cop stopping directly between the garage wall and the swimming pool, the white cop squeezing between the other garage wall and thick row of forsythia Victor had planted years ago to blot out the sight of his neighbor's yard, in particular a bare patch in the lawn created by the ceaseless ranging of an ugly black mongrel chained to a doghouse there. The dog barked all day long, "at everything that moves," as Janice had phrased it, but was quiet now, with a lunatic in plain view.

The man lay down on the peak of the roof and began to feel his way clumsily backward. Then he sat up and began to inch his way down, toward the black policeman, who encouraged his descent with friendly patter.

"That's right, Jackie. This way Roy won't be so hard on you. That's good, you're doing fine. Just a few more feet now."

When the man reached the edge of the roof, he looked down cautiously and then with frightening nimbleness—Janice gasped and her fingers dug into Victor's arm—hurled himself off, spun around in the air and landed squarely on his feet. The black cop grabbed him at once.

"Good work, Jackie boy! Now let's go home. Roy!" he called. "It's O.K. now."

But the man shrugged off the black policeman's grasp and walked away. Roy emerged from beyond the garage now, and it seemed to Victor he was actually holstering his gun. The man suddenly changed direction and marched toward the house. Janice gave a little squeal and slammed inside, but Victor was stricken by curiosity, rooted to the spot. The two policemen grabbed the man about four feet from Victor, one on each arm. The man tilted his head to one side and looked at Victor with terrible interest for a moment, and then asked, "Water? Please?"

"We got plenty of water at the station," Roy said.

"I don't mind getting him a glass of water," Victor said.

"We'll take care of that as soon as we're squared away," the black officer said, steering the man toward the driveway again, as though herding a cow.

The man looked over his shoulder at Victor as the officers hustled him along, and then disappeared around the corner of the house. Victor walked to the end of the driveway and watched the policemen install him in the back seat and then drive off.

Inside, he found Janice at the breakfast bar in the kitchen, trembling, and holding an awfully large tumbler of Scotch. "Darling, it's all right now." He tried to comfort her with a hug, but she pulled away.

"I don't believe you," she said. "You would have let him in the house."

"He didn't seem so terrible," Victor said.

"I just don't believe you." Janice was so frightened her lips were blue and her hands were shaking. The ice cubes in her drink gently tintinnabulated. "Don't you know what's going on out there? Don't you read anything but the business pages?"

"He was just a sad, miserable lump of a thing."

"But possibly quite dangerous. Did you see how he jumped down from the roof?"

"I had no intention of letting him in the house," Victor said. "I would have put the water on the little table and let him come and get it."

"He's obviously a lot stronger than he looks," Janice said. "And possibly not so dumb, either. And you're treating him like an ordinary houseguest."

"He wasn't armed. He was far away." Victor spoke matter-of-factly.

"Did you hear the sound he made?"

"Of course," Victor said. "He seemed so sad."

"Sad!" Janice laughed. "He sounded sick, and very . . . disturbed. Yes, disturbed."

"He's gone now," Victor said. "You can relax now, darling."

"He'll be back," Janice said.

"Don't be childish."

"You heard what the police said. He's done this before."

"Yes, but he's clearly harmless. They didn't exactly manacle him like some psychotic now, did they?"

"It could happen." Janice drank deeply.

"You're just being hysterical," Victor said.

"Goddamn it, Victor! If there had been no one out there, I might agree with you. But my God, there he was!"

"Finish your drink and we'll go to bed," Victor said.

"Not me. I'm not sleeping tonight."

"You'll just make things worse for yourself, staying up late, drinking too much."

"I'm not sleeping," Janice insisted. "Not tonight, not ever."

"And I'm not going to play along," Victor said. "I've got to be in town tomorrow, and I've got meetings, and I'm going to be there fresh and rested."

Sometime later Victor woke with a start as Janice slipped into bed beside him. The smell of the drinks annoyed him profoundly, and he turned away, drifted back into his dreams.

It was not, strictly speaking, true that Victor had to work in the morning. He could just as easily have conducted his business over the telephone, but he enjoyed being downtown and checking in with his broker and getting out of the house, away from Janice. He knew all this was a bad sign, and he had tried to think what the matter was and what he should do about it, but had also convinced himself it was just a phase, that it would pass and Janice and their relationship would return to normal in a little while. Besides, it was good for a man to get out into the world and see people, get the feel of things, talk to people who knew about this and that. He was looking forward to lunch at the new Antoine's with some of the traders at Chafee and Marks, and what conceivable good would it do to loiter around the house while Janice nursed her hangover and repented and went through all that tiresome business?

Janice herself, Victor reasoned, she was the one who would have to turn things around, take charge of whatever was bedeviling her. And if things got worse before they got better, he guessed he had plenty of patience. More than that, he felt he really didn't need her much now, for anything. He was loyal, but he was not dependent. The question of love didn't seem very significant any more, and even if it took a lover to renew Janice, Victor wouldn't mind, really wouldn't, he decided, as long as it didn't extend to divorce and disturb his assets.

It was not—was it?—that he didn't care. He did, he told himself, he did want Janice to improve herself, and the last thing she needed was a shock like that of last night. Damn it! She had been growing paranoid anyway and having some nut peering in the windows and clambering over the garage was most untimely. It fed into Janice's fears. She'd be a while getting the incident into perspective, Victor supposed, and then his mind turned again to his money and he was much happier.

He was going to sell off his steel and get into solar chips, and maybe ethanol, depending on what was floating. He also wanted to see what he could find out about a couple of little ceramic companies that might be going public soon, too. Some Japanese investors had already been nosing around, he had heard, and he could not stand the idea that they might be getting into this field first. He had plenty to keep him busy downtown, and by the time he returned home Janice might even be more relaxed. She would have had plenty of time to pull herself together and they might even enjoy a reasonably nice dinner. Janice knew how to do things right when she had a mind for it. After that, he could go off to his study as usual, and she could do what she liked—rent a movie or something, drive out to the mall—anything at all.

Victor's broker, Oliver George, was pleased to see him and had plenty to report. Oliver squinted, scratched his close-cropped beard spangled with gray, adjusted his glasses constantly. He was of the opinion that it might not, after all, be a good idea to dump the steel. The way Oliver saw it, the market was in for a real beating, soon, and he thought Victor should think about "survivability." He liked the long-range prospects of ceramics and ethanol, yes, but he didn't believe the little companies were going to weather the storm ahead, and there was really no way to predict which little guys would swim and which ones drown. Oliver also wanted nothing whatsoever to do with investing in computers or software companies, which he saw as a "crapshoot."

"Let's look at Japan," Oliver said.

"No," Victor said, "let's not. I want my money to stay right here, in this country."

"O.K.," Oliver said. "Let's not. Let's not look at China, either."

"Definitely not," Victor said.

"All I was thinking of," Oliver said, "was getting your assets out from the epicenter of what's coming."

"You're really that scared?" Victor asked.

"Don't put your house on the market," Oliver said. "I mean it. Don't build any condos. I predict real estate is going to get splattered, too. I don't see many safe havens out there, Victor. I think the choices are really quite limited now."

"That hasn't been my impression," Victor said, and he and Oliver launched into a debate, interrupted by several telephone calls, that was to last all morning. In the end, Victor had prevailed. He dumped the steel. He bought ethanol and ceramics and put some cash in the bank, intending soon to purchase a couple of CDs.

At Antoine's he met Gary "Tiger" Moran, who had earned his nickname from ferocious handball tactics, and Bill Donati, who had done very well for his clients in newsprint and wire. Moran was tall and blond with smoky gray eyes and a perpetual cynical smile. Donati seemed always to be brooding, but was really quite unpredictable and could be outrageously funny and gossip wickedly. He frequently delivered comic pronouncements from beneath his dark eyebrows, and Victor had always felt that here was a man who didn't understand his success and didn't think he deserved it. Moran, on the other hand, seemed to believe himself gifted, a cut above, and deserving of every lucky thing that came his way.

Victor liked these men and trusted them about as far as he could throw Trump Tower. They were great entertainment, but you had to be on your toes around them. They took very great satisfaction in seeing you swallow a lie. "They would put butter on it and feed it to you on a golden spoon" was how Oliver had described their tactics. "They'd just as soon be the last investors on earth." They also, occasionally, dropped very interesting little tidbits of market news.

Today, however, they had nothing particularly stunning to reveal. They said they did not agree with Oliver's downbeat assessment of the market's immediate future and went on to something that interested them more: who the biggest grossing athletes were and what they were doing with their incomes. As far as they were concerned, anybody with any smarts could stay ahead of the market readjustments that new technologies and world progress would require.

"It's bad habits that kill everybody," Donati said. "Not bad luck."

"Stay loose," Moran said. "That's the key."

"These profundities have just cost you the price of the lunch." Donati handed Victor the bill.

"Bullshit," Victor said nobly. He passed the bill to Moran.

"Even Steven," Moran said, after cursory study, "it's about twenty-three bucks apiece."

Victor was a little disappointed by the luncheon, but decided to have another drink at the bar after the traders left. He opened the polarized glass doors to the bar, wishing he had put a few thousand into this product, for he was seeing it now in all the new automobiles and in yacht cabins, and somebody was cleaning up on it. He actually hated its use in car windows because you could never tell if someone saw you approaching or not, but he was angry with himself that he hadn't seen its profit potential.

Inside, his attention was immediately galvanized by two striking women who, with long, slender fingers, were tapping ashes into the tray before them and laughing with splendid abandon. They were sharing a bottle of champagne and gave every appearance of celebrating some success. Victor chose a seat close enough to eavesdrop on them but without seeming to intrude. If Moran and Donati had been with him, they would certainly have found a way to insinuate themselves into the women's conversation and celebration, but Victor was too shy for that and he even found the beauty and the polish of the two women a little intimidating. They were both blond and wore dresses that hugged their figures and showed off their shapely legs. Their eyes glowed, their complexions gleamed, and their smiles flashed rows of perfect white teeth. They were buxom and sleek. They could have been models, and sisters, but in fact their conversation was quite a technical one about principles of physics that Victor was only able to follow in the most general sort of way. Apparently, he decided, they were engineers.

It took him the time of one drink to understand that the women were involved in selling weapons to the American military. They had just returned from a convention in Washington, D.C., where they had apparently made a terrific deal or two and survived some tremendous partying. They were gorgeous, Victor thought, and they were giddy with success. He wondered what it would be like to attend a party with a pair of gorgeous predators like these, women who could describe to you the action of a missile or the latest developments in automatic weapons, in engineering terms, and who would think nothing of opening, as the tallest of the two was doing now, another and then another button at the bustline of their dresses.

Victor had to look away. Things were going on in this world which he would never know about. Surely someone climbed in bed with beauties like these. He thought of Janice now, getting soft, deteriorating into some kind of awful, inhibiting fear that had begun to shut down both their lives, and he felt frightened himself now. Something about these women frightened him more, far more than even the lunatic he had encountered the night before.

The shorter of the two women spoke to Victor, with a little laugh. "Hey, guy." She held up a glass and her green eyes glittered merrily. "A little champagne?"

Victor bolted from the bar, followed by a squeal of dismay and outraged female laughter. The damned polarized glass doors were heavy and slow to let him through, and he resented them, the slight resistance they offered to his will to be gone from the presence of those sirens. Jesus, he thought, the cynicism of it, using tits and ass to get the attention of the generals. But then he mocked himself for his Puritanism, which he knew was insincere. He wasn't stupid. He knew what competition was; and he knew that in ten years the women celebrating in the bar would probably not have been kicked upstairs but would be doing something else, selling something else, or going soft, too. He didn't really begrudge them their champagne, begrudge them anything, and he knew it wasn't scruples propelling him back onto the street. He could rub shoulders with arms merchants. If his ethanol and ceramics companies landed military contracts, he would break out the champagne, too. He hadn't made the world and he wasn't responsible for its savagery.

But God they had frightened him!

Driving the freeway home, Victor could not understand himself and his own behavior. He was deeply irritated with himself, on the one hand, for passing up a chance to meet those women. On the other, he supposed—and the supposition itself was dispiriting—that he would only have been teased and dropped the minute someone younger, quicker of wit, handsomer, who knew the rules of the games, came along. Beauties like that would take scant interest in him. By escaping so quickly he was just being realistic. Why torture himself for nothing?

And yet: what was he going home to? He might at least have enjoyed the repartee in the bar and had those beautiful smiles and open buttons to think about as he fell asleep that night. Instead there was just the usual, and a bored, obviously unhappy and too often frightened wife awaiting him. And, of course, his portfolio which he now would have to update: new entries, new hopes there.

He pulled into the garage and hit the switch on the dashboard which lowered the doors automatically, slowly behind him. He remembered the fleeting impression of last night, how the interior of the car had seemed so peaceful inside the garage, and he lingered a moment to savor it now. He could see why people might choose such a spot to end it, the car engine murmuring them along to a dozing death. A last peaceful moment. Terrible idea, Victor shuddered, and then the wail of that lunatic filled his mind: nothing peaceful about that, was there?

Victor gathered his newspapers and briefcase and made sure the garage door was locked as he stepped outside. He glanced up at the garage peak, which normally would never have even entered his consciousness, and remembered the black policeman saying, *Oh, Jackie likes to climb.* What in God's name was that all about? Talk about things in this world you could never understand!

Or could you? Victor moved an empty glass on the table beside the pool to make room for his paraphernalia and walked to the rear of the garage. His painting ladders were there, rungs stained with the buckskin and redwood brown he had used to touch up some of the trim a while ago. The lunatic had leaned the lightest of these against the back wall of the garage and somehow mounted the gable from there. Victor thought it must have taken considerable strength, and some balance, to haul himself onto the roof from that angle.

He made sure the ladder was firmly planted, then climbed several steps, and then several steps more. He found that he could balance against the back wall, his feet on the penultimate rung, and actually see over the edge of the roof. The dark blue shingles rippled away like water. He cupped his hands over the gable and began to haul himself up, until his feet came free of the ladder and he had no choice now but to plunge forward and kick and haul himself, haul his own suddenly awful weight onto the rough, biting surface. He lay on his belly like a snake with his feet dangling over the edge, panted as the man must have done, but actually on the roof. The neighbor's dog heralded the feat with a paroxysm of snarls and yelps. The shingles were rough on Victor's cheek, but quite warm, and he actually enjoyed lying there. From his vantage now, the pool seemed to come right in under the eaves, into the garage itself.

He drew his legs up and steadied himself, and edged forward with the gable between his feet. The man might have rolled his way along, Victor thought. He seemed to like rolling. Victor tried a roll or two and the sky and then the shingles, sky and shingles, a cloud and shiny blue flakes crossed his consciousness. When he came to the spot where the man had sat and dangled his feet, he sat, too, and dangled his legs over the peak.

The view was really quite pleasant. He could see into the second story and attic windows of his own house, and although he was not so distant from the ground after all, the little odds and ends around his house seemed small, and to have been disarranged almost artfully. The neighbor's dog seemed small and huffy, and the neighborhood itself lay before him like a convoy of ships moving slowly across an almost placid sea. Victor felt released from any identity with all this, like an alien come down to attempt a closer understanding of all those points of light in the darkness of the earth, or the squares and triangles and the curving lines between light and light, circle and square. They were certainly a busy species, whoever they were out there, Victor imagined.

One difference between the lunatic and himself, however, was that the man had been naked, or nearly so. Absently,

Victor unstrung his tie and peeled off his jacket and dropped them separately to the ground below. The jacket fell on the tie like a hawk on a snake, but did not fly off with its kill. Victor had started on the buttons of his shirt when Janice, holding a drink, stumbled through the back door. She shielded her eyes with her free hand, winced up at Victor a moment, and then cried out:

"What in God's name are you doing up there? Victor! Why are you doing this to me?"

"Oh, be quiet!" Victor said, coming slowly to his senses, but regretting also the dissipation of the mood, the seeming rectitude of the mood he had just experienced. "Can't you see I'm trying to fix something up here? What else could I possibly be up here for, but to make repairs?"

Commander of the Buffaloes

The 104th Transportation Company was moved in May of 1942 from the West Coast to a tiny town in Missouri about halfway between Hannibal and St. Louis. Though the Army supplied no reasons, the troops, all black, assumed the recent attack on Pearl Harbor had alerted someone that coastal installations might be imperiled by Japanese air raid, if not also by Nazi submarine. The tanks were moved by rail, but the trucks, most of them, were driven in a near fiasco of lost drivers, a green caravan by day, a file of cat's-eye headlights by night, rumbling across the southwestern deserts until it reached that ancient artery of transportation, the Mississippi River. And thus the Army, in its wisdom, placed the 104th Buffaloes at the mercy of Ridgevale.

Sam Bertram, company clerk of the Buffaloes, as the 104th was called, was still grieving about the move when the white sheriff showed up in the day room and asked, or rather demanded, to speak to Captain Arnold. Sam and his desk interposed between the impatient sheriff and his commanding officer, and Sam, lethargic still with grief at having moved from the delights of Los Angeles to this cracker town in Nowhere, Missouri—Ridgevale, for God's sake—shifted a few unpacked boxes around before he took up the sheriff's "request" in earnest.

"Did you hear me, boy?"

"I heard you," Sam said. "Please state the nature of your business with the Captain."

"I'm sort of a welcoming committee." The sheriff exuded a quick, self-satisfied chuckle, then regarded Sam with compelling insolence.

"Name, sir?"

"Keets. Bill Keets."

Sam glanced away now, out of habit, and not having any particular desire to let the sheriff ruffle him. He stepped around the partition behind him and into the Captain's lair.

"A Sheriff Keets is out front, sir. He wants to talk to you."

Arnold dropped his feet from the desk and carefully placed a cigar in the ashtray on the windowsill. The window looked out across a bald field to a row of corrugated steel sheds where the company's trucks were stored and being repaired and readied for shipment into combat. Sam couldn't look out, much less walk out into the new base without feeling a shock of hurt. Things had been so fine in L.A., just so, so fine.

"Send him in, I guess." Arnold folded his blue-white hands on the desk and gave Sam a look of unconscious despair, probably not so much for the recent move as for his hangover. Captain had a lot of problems, only white man on the post, "and not your basic Whiz Kid," as Sam's ally, Mo Henderson, had put it. Troop morale had bottomed out, too, and a speech the Captain had given that morning to reassure the men the move had been a tactical necessity crucial to the war effort only deepened the malaise. Everyone's misery being what it was, Sam didn't feel sorry for the Captain at all. He didn't feel much of anything for Arnold, who apparently repaid the compliment as long as Sam did his work and kept things running smoothly.

"Captain will see you, Sheriff." Sam didn't look at the man

and the sheriff said nothing as he ambled, butt-heavy with nightstick and pistol, into the Captain's office.

No matter how much work was staring him in the face at the moment, Sam knew very well he could not miss the conversation that was about to transpire in Arnold's office and he positioned himself just outside the door with clipboard in hand. Mo had observed long ago that a man with a clipboard, even a black man, could go anywhere in the Army without being questioned, and in this case the clipboard contained a report that Arnold would eventually need to sign. Protected thus with official business at the ready, Sam put his ear to the door.

Ridgevale, he heard Sheriff Keets explain, had become a little anxious about the Buffaloes, the law of the region being what it was. His sworn duty being to uphold that law, Keets had come to inquire whether the Army could, therefore, provide transportation for soldiers returning from leave at night, inasmuch as the bus station was to the east of Ridgevale and the base to the west? Arnold received the inquiry with calm disgust, and it was easy for Sam to imagine the Captain's neck turning ruddy red as it did whenever a decision was required.

After a few intervening questions and some banter, Arnold said that no, Army vehicles could not be used to transport personnel on leave but that he would take the town's anxiety to heart and limit the number of men he sent on leave so that Ridgevale would never have reason to fear a colored invasion of its borders. He would also, he affirmed, but Sam doubted he would have the courage for it, notify the troops that Ridgevale was off limits after sundown.

The sheriff was grateful for these considerations but still concerned that black soldiers might be deposited along the highway after dark and grow eager to seek shelter from rain or cold, or desire to relieve physical discomfort or sleepiness by passing through Ridgevale to the base.

"I'll make sure, then," Arnold said, "that all leave time will end at sundown on the last day. That will take care of that."

Sam knew better about this, too. The world did not run according to Captain Arnold's orders. It never had, and it never would. If the truth were known, not even the 104th Buffaloes ran according to Arnold's orders, but in spite of them.

Discouraged already, Sam was now angry. He conveyed the news to astonished barracks mates that night. Mo was especially vehement in his declarations of disgust, and he wondered aloud (again) whether he just ought to go AWOL for good, get so deep in the Tennessee hills they would never find him. His voice was rumbling low, ministerial in tone, though Mo himself did not exactly express himself in ecclesiastical language regarding the present offense. He was very dark, broad-shouldered, of powerful build, with high cheekbones that bespoke some mixture of Indian heritage. Sam knew Mo to be a fundamentally gentle person, but the service had made him cynical and people began properly to fear his recent brooding. On the trip from California he had attempted to desert, but was quickly arrested, in Texas, where he had gone to see a brother. After a week in the brig he was returned to duty a buck private, a status he endured with sullen quietude. Sam had been trying recently to cheer him up, but his efforts, though Mo appreciated them, were having scant success. The brooding continued; Mo's meanness deepened. His declaration of plans to go AWOL again was debated, scoffed at, then encouraged.

"Treat you like a damned dog," Mo declared. "It's called serving your country."

In the end, all the debate accomplished was to confirm the

fact that every weekend leave to St. Louis would terminate in the early afternoon, and a one-day pass was rendered almost meaningless since there was no city close enough for anyone to bus to it and then do anything else but return at once in order to beat the curfew.

In the weeks that followed, the Buffaloes were to learn another gloomy fact: the order to stay out of Ridgevale after dark put the soldiers completely at the mercy of the Green Valley Bus Line, whose machinery was in constant disrepair and whose drivers had no more respect for the published timetables than for the blacks, whether uniformed or not, who entered their doors. Inevitably, the bus arrived late, after the sun had set, and inevitably the soldiers had tried to find obscure passages through town—via back streets or farmers' fields—and suffered arrest. Keets was very vigilant at night, and hired deputies whose understanding of the rights of the arrested or accused was less than sophisticated. You were lucky to be jailed without being beaten on the way, and then charged with resisting arrest.

Arnold was not helpful with this problem. The fines of the soldiers who were jailed were paid by the other soldiers. Arnold was at least mild in his disciplining of offenders, if and when he remembered the sheriff's complaints and threats to take the growing problem to a higher command. The Captain was not defying the white man's law by foot-dragging or non-cooperation, as Sam well knew. He was simply enduring his exile from mainstream career progress by the traditional military means of such men: the bottle. The sheriff and his complaints were just another nuisance to him, a problem which, if Arnold solved it, would not enhance his paycheck or his status in the ranks one iota. Having no other resources and little imagination, Arnold was happy to rot where he was, and

Sam's instructions were, however neatly phrased, to make that as comfortable as possible. Sam obliged. It made his own life that much easier with Arnold out of his hair.

Meanwhile, as long as the trucks were repaired and shipped, Arnold had little to do with the day-to-day operations, and Sam was unofficially in charge. He accepted this role because more than anything it spared him from boredom, and it challenged him in a way that nothing else ever had. He wasn't sticking his neck out for Arnold, just keeping things flowing. Nothing was done without Arnold's signature authorizing it; and if Arnold was signing orders he hadn't even read, that was his worry, not Sam's. Whenever Arnold did, in fact, try to assert himself with the Buffaloes, he usually created snafus and confusion. Better when he sits behind that frosted glass and sips his gin and water, Sam thought. Easier for everybody that way.

One weekend Sam and Mo took the Green Valley ("Gee Vee," troops called it) bus to St. Louis and raised general hell for about twenty-four hours. They were in full debauch when the necessity of climbing aboard GV again to beat the curfew struck, and they sped to the bus station in a state of frustration, surprised at how rapidly the hours had passed. They sat as far back in the musty seats as possible, and in a kind of sullen defiance of regulations and the driver (who pretended not to notice) passed a pint of Old Crow back and forth between them.

The trip, scheduled to last three hours and fifteen minutes, was already four hours old and the bus twenty miles from Ridgevale when it broke down. Sam and Mo took the opportunity to trudge off into a stand of nearby woods to relieve themselves, then returned to watch the driver tinker with an engine he obviously had no understanding of. The breakdown was the company's fault, of course, according to the driver.

What the hell could he do? The passengers milled along the roadside while the driver fiddled some more and one of the young white boys hiked off in search of a telephone.

"If we don't get this show on the road," Mo grumbled, "we're goin' to be all night long walkin' around that damned Ridgevale."

"You fix the goddamn bus then," Sam said in disgust. The prospect of waiting the night out on Ridgevale's borders burned his heart.

"Maybe I will." Mo made his way into the circle of people amusing themselves by watching the frustrations of the driver, and after a little observation knelt down beside the man and offered some suggestions on how to find out what was wrong and what to do about it. The driver, clearly reluctant to take instructions from a nigger, nevertheless was frustrated enough to try any damn-fool thing, and to accept a little help, which Mo little by little provided, until he too was elbow-deep in the engine, cleaning spark plugs and blowing through fuel lines, adjusting the carburetor and making other basic repairs. About an hour later, the engine banged and popped and started. The passengers, some of whom nodded thanks to Mo as he tried vainly to wipe the grease and oil off his hands with a tiny handkerchief, boarded the bus, and the journey continued.

"Fuel pump's goin'," Mo confided to Sam as they settled in again. "Might make it to Ridgevale, though."

But when the Green Valley bus coughed up to the Ridgevale stop, the sun was already behind the hills. Sam and Mo stepped down to the road and watched the bus shudder away. Mo kicked stones for a while and Sam fumed and cursed. His head hurt from the booze, he was tired from lack of sleep, and he cursed Ridgevale aloud for keeping him from his bed.

"Jesus, be quiet!" Mo commanded. "You'll have the crackers

comin' out after you, hollerin' like that. They probably check on every bus that stops out here."

Sam swore and sat down hard by the side of the road. "Man, it makes me so tired," he said.

"I know it."

"I don't want to sleep out here in a damn ditch."

"At least it ain't rainin'," Mo said.

"The hell it ain't," Sam said. "It's rainin' like a dog. Can't you feel it?"

"No," Mo said. "I'm countin' stars."

"Well, it sure as hell is rainin'," Sam said, rising to his feet, "and I'm damned if I'm sittin' out here gettin' soaked."

"You're drunk and you're crazy," Mo said. "And where in hell do you think you're goin'?"

"I'm gettin' out of this rain," Sam said. "I'm goin' to the base."

"You fool!" Mo said. "Sheriff will grab your ass in a minute over there."

"I hope he does," Sam asserted. "The way I feel, I just might puke in his lap."

"Goddamn it." Mo grabbed Sam's sleeve. "At least let's not go through the main street. We can head up over the hill there and cut down through the orchard, then go along by the creek."

"That's the long way around," Sam insisted.

"But the way you're goin'," Mo said, biting each word with clenched teeth, "doesn't go to the base. It goes to the jail."

This remark persuaded Sam, and though it galled him to go through Ridgevale like a coyote, he knew he would rather do that than sleep in a field or in Ridgevale's infamous jail. But both he and Mo were about to become aware of another fact: Sheriff Keets had hired for the evening a pair of young men who were particularly ardent on the subject of black curfew.

And when Sam and Mo labored down from the little dirt road that would take them from the orchard and then to the creek which they would follow to the base, car headlights flicked on, caught them in its beams, and they were stabbed by a spotlight and commanded to halt.

"The hell!" Sam started to bolt, but Mo grabbed him and muttered, "Shotguns. They got shotguns, man."

Sam closed his eyes against the white light, bit his tongue so hard that it broke and bled. Two shadows sauntered up through the lights, and Sam heard one of the deputies chuckling low.

"Now look at this shit, will you, Danny."

"Guess these boys can't read a lick, and signs on every road. Say, can you boys read?"

And it was Mo, not Sam, who leapt first into the glare, and hit with such force that the shape slipped off into the darkness like a stone going down in water. Sam did not hesitate, sprang pantherlike, felt the iron in his teeth, and still clawed forward, and down, striking the ground out of the blaze of light, could see the straining, scared face of the man before he struck it and his hand went numb. The fight was desperately quiet, but soon over, a mistake they paid for as they sat cuffed together in the car, taking random blows from the deputies, gloves filled with bullets, until Sam's consciousness lifted off like a crow rising from carrion.

Late the next afternoon a Sergeant Haywood showed up to check on the condition of Sam and Mo and to negotiate their release. The sheriff had been adamant that Arnold himself show up to see just what the situation was coming to, niggers attacking his sworn officers, but Arnold had been just as adamant about not coming into town.

"Captain says he's not interfering with the law. Captain also says that if the sheriff wants to see him, the sheriff has a car he can drive to the base."

"You tell the Captain I'm not drivin' all over the county on his orders."

"It's no orders," Haywood said evenly. "And you got a telephone, so tell him yourself."

Keets fumed. "All I get any more is smartass talk."

"I'm just doing my job," Haywood said.

"You're a messenger boy, aren't you?"

"No, sir, I came to get these men out of jail."

"They're not goin' anywhere. We've thrown the book at 'em. They're going to stand trial."

"No, sir," Haywood said. "I got the papers right here. They're going to the base hospital. If you don't like the papers, you can argue with Captain Arnold and the Army lawyer, not me."

"You're just a smartass like all the rest of the newcomers," Keets said, snapping the papers from Haywood and waddling into his office. He shut the door, and Haywood stepped over to the cell where Sam and Mo were sitting side by side on the lower bunk.

"Somebody whipped your ass." Haywood smiled and leaned against the bars. "Arnold ain't here really," he said quietly, "because the base is about in an uproar over you guys. Cats was loading up trucks with tire irons, just foaming to come into town. Captain's running his ass off trying to keep the lid on. Keets doesn't let you out, you might see a lot of AWOL Buffaloes shopping at the general store this afternoon."

"Christ Almighty!" Mo said.

"Now you know why Arnold is skimpy on those passes. Suppose it was six of you last night, and not just two." He pointed to Sam. "You get anything for that head cut yet, bro? You need to get that cleaned up."

"They didn't give us shit," Sam said.

That evening Sam and Mo were back on base, under military arrest and confined to barracks. A stream of friends had been in and out, telling them about the near riot that had taken place on the base. Captain Arnold, of course, had seen the two men as soon as they arrived and had been nearly hysterical in condemnation of their actions, telling them that harmony with the town was essential to the functioning of the base, and that because of their actions he was considering canceling all leaves in the future to avoid such inflammatory confrontations. Yes, the soldiers on the base were hot under the collar about the incident; but so were the people of Ridgevale, and unless a solution was found, nobody was going to be safe, day or night.

The Captain screamed on about their lack of foresight on the consequences of their actions and promised they would pay for it not only in civilian court, but on the base, too. Oh, he had learned a lesson. He'd been too lax. He had imagined he could trust Sam. And they had just about started a war. The operations of the Buffaloes were important, and they had jeopardized them by their reckless actions.

Sam and Mo had weathered this verbal assault, and then Arnold dismissed Mo, confining him to hospital barracks, under guard, until further notice. But Sam he kept in his office, allowed him to sit down, and then collapsed in his own chair, obviously weary, and one of his eyes twitched nervously.

"O.K., Sam," he said. "What is it you want?"

"Me?"

"The men on the base. What do you want? I mean to keep this thing from exploding. And understand Ridgevale's curfew will not be revoked."

"That's what we want."

"That can't happen. What else can we do?"

"Who's 'we,' Captain?"

"You, me, Ridgevale, Keets."

"I don't know," Sam said. "My head hurts."

"You're lucky to be alive. You know that? Be glad you can feel your head at all."

Be glad? Sam thought he was going to be sick, but he smiled. "If we have to wait over there, give us a place to wait, not just a ditch. But a shelter. A place to sit down. With lights. And a latrine. A table."

"We could build that, but maybe we'd have to buy land."

"And if it's late, can't you get us across town some way?"

"I can't authorize vehicles for that."

"What about a damn taxi? In L.A. we could always grab a cab."

"All right," Arnold said. "I'll take it up with Keets. Somebody out there shouldn't mind making a few bucks taxiing you men." He dismissed Sam then, confining him with Mo to hospital barracks, but ordering him also to appear for duty in the morning.

"You're not goin' to bust me, Captain?"

"No," Arnold said, twisting away from him in his chair. "Not yet."

Sam looked at the back of the Captain's head and felt sad, not just for himself but for Arnold's cowardice and ineptitude, his lack of inspiration for enduring anything but the status quo. Yes, better lock me up, he thought. I did want to kill somebody. I really did.

The men who visited Sam and Mo that evening reported that some sort of meeting was in progress at headquarters. State and town police cars ringed the building and all sorts of white shirts and ties were parading in and out of it.

"Guess they're runnin' scared," Lou Hazen opined. "Guess they would not like to see any niggers get shot up here."

"Or white folks," Mo said with a dark laugh.

"Could be that, too," Lou said, nodding gravely.

The results of the meeting and the combined wisdom of

the establishment manifested itself in the following weeks. The bus was now authorized to stop at one of Ridgevale's gas stations, and an outhouse had been constructed behind that institution for the soldiers' use. A taxi company also sprang up, the proprietor and sole operator being one Kevin Keets, the sheriff's brother. Just off the gas station parking area, a shed was erected, combining a one-room office for the taxi company with telephone and filing cabinet, and a waiting room for its only customers.

This solution to the preservation of Ridgevale's curfew custom and the needs of the 104th Buffaloes was heralded as great and humanitarian and fond hopes were expressed that it would put an end to the tension between the town and the base.

"Right," Mo said. "Now we can drink co'colas and take a crap while we wait for the sheriff's brother to overcharge us for a five-mile ride."

On the base itself, the soldiers regarded the new arrangements as barely tolerable. Kevin Keets worked when he felt like it, and often would refuse to take individual soldiers through town to the base, preferring to wait until he had a carload of passengers. His rates were arbitrary, growing steeper with the passengers' desperation to return to base before regulation deadlines. Kevin also made himself famous, or infamous, for the lectures he imposed on his clients while he chauffeured them, on America and its traditions, on manhood, on tradition and the Bible, on law and justice, and sometimes less ethereal topics such as the making of moonshine, the correct use of corncobs, and how great it was to see the little yellow bastards finally getting their asses whipped in the Pacific. These lectures were frequently the subject of barracks humor, and vitriol.

"Was Kevin in the pulpit again as usual?"

"I don't listen to his bullshit."

"He was talkin' about the animal kingdom, how God made it."

"Did Kevin talk to God first?"

"I believe so."

"Where'd we fit in?"

"About on the level of the orangutans."

"He must be getting liberalized. Last year it was on the level of dogs."

"Wouldn't swear to that. I believe Kevin likes dogs more'n people."

"Where'd he get his license to preach that trash?"

"From the sheriff. Who else?"

"You don't listen to him, he'll throw you out in the street in the middle of the night and call the cops."

"He won't throw me out, and if they find him runnin' around some night with no goddamn tongue in his head, you just keep quiet, hear?"

"It's true, goddammit. Someday somebody is going to be ridin' with Kevin who is drunk and mean and he'll start on his bullshit once too often, and smack."

Kevin, oblivious to the hatred he inspired, continued his harangues for another year, just as the town, oblivious to the contempt it had earned from the soldiers, continued to deny their existence. Now that the western shores were again deemed safe, however, and the war in the Pacific was entering an accelerated phase, the 104th Buffaloes were ordered to strike the base at Ridgevale and return to Los Angeles. Everyone on the base was joyful, except Captain Arnold, who confided to Sam that he would not be going to Los Angeles again. Instead, the Army was sending him to New Jersey, into an even lesser post than the one he now held, a railroad depot assignment where his main task would be to keep records.

"The men who saw action will be getting the plums, of

course." Arnold sipped his gin and water, no longer interested in keeping his habit secret from his staff and the men on the base. "I got about six more years to do and then I can go in for early retirement. Won't be much, at my pay. Aw, what the hell," he shrugged, sipped, ordered Sam to carry on, automatically signed the papers Sam passed under his nose.

These papers, had Arnold cared to look at them, contained orders Sam himself had cut, with the help of Mo and a little whiskey and a barracks trip down memory lane through all the bitter moments they had suffered at the hands of the little town that hosted and apparently hated them. The orders went out and down the line and no one questioned them or asked Arnold to confirm them or sent them back as a patent joke. They were received, the trucks rumbled out, a tractor loaded with two bulldozers, two four-by-fours, a six-by-six, and assorted working crew in troop transports, the last remnants of the 104th Transportation Company's fleet, soon to join the convoy to Los Angeles.

Arnold himself was already aboard a DC-3 headed for Cincinnati and then New Jersey where the news of the successful completion of his last commands would reach him.

Kevin Keets was at the gas station door when the tractor trailer pulled up at the taxi office and, one after another, two yellow bulldozers lumbered down the ramp. At first Kevin thought the goddamn niggers were too stupid to drive the machines, because one came dangerously close to smashing the taxi and the other seemed headed for the office itself. By the time he was out the door of the gas station, however, he realized that, in fact, the operators were quite expertly razing every vestige of his business, and with exquisite timing: no sooner had the outhouse been smashed to splinters than the taxi was crunched and scraped into the pit below, where it sank up to its windows in sludge. Kevin was instantly at the telephone for the sheriff, but his efforts were futile because across town the sheriff was having problems of his own.

At that moment, the county jail was being turned to rubble by a Walker Bulldog, which systematically caved in the corners of the cinderblock structure and then, under its accordion steel tread, battered the sheriff's cruiser to something resembling a rumpled tin can. Keets and his deputy heard their bullets whine from the tank's turret, but could do nothing to stop the machine. The cannon arced through the plate-glass windows, tore out the front entrance emblazoned with the Ridgevale County seal and the winged automobile tire that was the region's symbol of the law. The tank then rumbled toward the former Buffalo base in a gray cloud of Missouri dust.

Kevin Keets, at the gas station, had his next telephone calls to the state police interrupted when he found it necessary to evacuate the building to save his own hide. He watched in a kind of furious awe as the bulldozer blades slashed into the glass wall across the front, then rumbled the metal sides of the building, puncturing them with enormous holes that closed slowly, like tired eyes, as the roof slowly collapsed into the repair bays and the former office.

The porch sitters at the general store, who might have been outraged at the show, had their own spectacle to behold. Two six-by-sixes stopped in the street out front, and a squad of black soldiers calmly went about seizing chains to the porch pillars. It did not take long for the rocking chairs and the interior of the building to be evacuated. The tires churned powerfully in the street, crunching cinders, and the pillars popped like matchsticks. The projecting roof creaked and cracked slowly down and the metal sign that had graced it for so many years, trembling and rattling like thunder, crashed through the wooden stairs.

Then the trucks rumbled away from the Mighty Mississippi

and when they joined the last portion of the convoy, which had awaited them in St. Louis, there was really no sure way to tell which drivers and which trucks had been so loyal to their Captain's last commands that they razed the village of Ridgevale and all those institutions which had so offended the Buffaloes.

"You just might catch hell on this one," Mo said to Sam as they jounced along in the front seat of a six-by.

"Let 'em hang me," Sam said. He squinted into the sunset before them, the sky exploding in bursts of purple and orange, and he thought it resembled the work of a cosmic bomber, frozen in time. He settled back. He couldn't wait to see L.A. again.

My Kline Syndrome

Moses Kline is my enemy, and I don't think he even knows it. Sometimes it seems I'm forever playing Salieri to his Mozart and I don't like it a bit.

It's my own fault, in a way. Karen pointed this out to me, not long, as a matter of fact, before she took up with Kline, to put it mildly. It's this thing I grew up with, the way I was raised, and it's been with me so long it seems like instinct. I hate to lose. And sometimes I even hate to lose when I'm really not losing: to me, being number two is the same as failure. To tell you the truth, when it comes to winning and losing, I'm not like the Japanese at all, I'm not the least bit happy with a tie. I want it settled.

Back in those days I feel Kline and me, one day, we're going out on the dusty street and draw six-guns. Man to man. The way you can't settle things any more. Thank God we didn't become lawyers, Kline and I. We could have given each other a lifetime of headaches.

Back then he thinks he's a gracious winner. I'm not used to losing at tennis, for example. When I was in Ohio, pre-med, I tore them all up, the doctors, the other students, the club pro —I whomped their butts. Kline came from even farther across the country than I did, from Stanford, and we shared duties on the night wards our first year out here, catching babies and taking samples from heart attack victims and scaring ourselves to death with what we didn't know. And one night, he asks me—innocently—do I play tennis?

"I play a little," I said. "I haven't been on the court in a while."

"Me, too," Kline said. "Do you think we could squeeze in a game sometime?"

"Jesus, I don't know," I said. "I barely have time enough to sleep."

"Saturday morning maybe?" Kline asked. And you know how he asked it. Forever innocent. Maybe he put those beautiful long fingers up against his jaw and tipped his head so his alert brown eyes got smothered a little by those authoritarian brows. Maybe he wasn't real clean-shaven at that late hour and looked a little vulnerable.

Besides, you know, I figured, I'm going to give this guy a shock.

He aced his first serve. Really. This almost never happened to me. I mean, I had to be hung over for that to happen, and I did a very fast reassessment.

"Sorry!" he said. Can you believe that?

From that moment on, it was a duel to the death. Sorry me, would he? And to my horror, my best shots came screaming back at me. We were into power hitting then. And goddamn it if I didn't lose. Kline jogs up to the net, grinning, his beautiful fingers extended for a handshake, lean and tall, a lady killer, I should have known. I give him a desultory shake and he slaps me on the back, says, "Anybody could have missed that shot."

Now the truth is, he was right, because the shot he made which put me away was a killer—it not only hit the perfect spot right inside the line, it hit there with more speed than I have ever seen on a tennis ball, ever, and this after nearly two hours of combat. McEnroe, Navratilova would have missed that shot. Connors would have thrown his racket at it. Lendl would have wrinkled his nose. But that's not what Kline was saying. He was pretending to be lucky.

Some people think losing at tennis is trivial. I don't now, and I didn't then. I don't separate things. I told you, I got this ingrained in me as a kid, and I still believe it: sports is life. Winning is winning. Losing by one point is losing.

Here's another case, a more serious one in some eyes. An old man comes into the ward about four-thirty in the morning, just when we're thinking we're finally going to be out of there in a little while and able to get some sleep. He's in terrible pain and he's foaming at the mouth, perspiring, fever, headache, nausea, terrible cramp in the upper intestinal area. Clearly he has also been out on a toot, because you can smell it all over him. He's delirious and we're not getting a clear picture of his problem, except we know it's not a heart attack, and we find his blood sugar is way off and for a minute Kline and I ask each other, was this guy poisoned? Is it salmonella? Or maybe diabetes-related—an old guy on a drunk who forgot his insulin?

Finally it hits me: "Pancreas," I say.

"Ruptured appendix," Kline says. "We can't play around. We've got to get in there and get it."

He phones Dr. Tillotson, the surgeon on call, and I take another vial of blood from the old man and shoot it down to the lab, because I'm positive it's pancreatic and I'm going to have the numbers to show Dr. Tillotson when she steams in. Besides, the location of the pain is not specific to the appendix, the guy is too old for appendix trouble, and, most important, it's the blood sugar level that clinches my case.

"What have we got?" Tillotson says when she strides in, pushing gray hair under the pale green cap, her eyeglasses glinting, then plunging into the sink.

"Ruptured appendix," Kline says.

"Pancreatitis," I say.

"What's on the chart?" Tillotson asks, and I run it down, very careful to stress the blood test results.

"Get his sugar level up," Tillotson commands. "We don't want to put this guy in shock. Then," she says, "we'll get his appendix out."

And Kline was right. It was an awful mess in there. Tillotson lectured us on referred pain—the kind of thing where you bring your kid to the doctor's office with nausea and stomach cramps and the dumb doctor immediately looks in the kid's ear. Pain travels. It sneaks around. I knew this. Kline knew it better.

It gets worse. Not the pain, but my Kline problem. There's this woman I like, Karen. I'm not in love with her, but I have my needs, and she is very beautiful and very interesting company. She appeals to me in a very basic way. I see her and I'm hungry. She's apparently pheromone dynamite. If you could have watched her play tennis for two minutes, you would have understood my attraction—she was a beautiful, alert, graceful, well-made, well-conditioned animal. When I thought about her, I was filled with a literally physical yearning. We also made each other laugh.

Her real name is Karen Greene, but for some reason everyone calls her Maggie. I met her at a retirement party for her father, Max Greene, formerly a surgeon, then the head of the hospital board here for fifteen years after he retired the knife. Karen-Maggie was a department store buyer and she traveled a lot, and she liked me enough to call me when she was in town, and we played tennis and we were getting close enough to discuss our sexual histories and assure each other (even then) that we were free of any of the age's horrifying viruses. (In those days the Big Scare was Herpes—oh age of innocence!) So it seemed the time was coming, and soon, when my prolonged misery of desiring might be ended in just the way I'd hoped with just the woman I'd wanted. The prospect of it brightened my days.

Then Karen-Maggie meets Kline-Mozart. It's not easy to talk about this even now, I hope you appreciate. Kline is cool. He's so goddamn cool. We were at a little party for the interns in our class, for which Kline has cooked a fish chowder that everyone seems to think is wonderful and to which I have brought strawberry blintzes from the local deli—which no one will eat because of hyper-cholesterol consciousness, as if they were actively poisonous.

You know that feeling of dread you get? I came out of the kitchen at one point and I saw Kline and Karen in a dark corner together, chatting in a too-animated way, smiling, seeming awfully comfortable with each other—the body language going on was just incredible. The dread came down from the top of my head and it kind of coated my body.

Kline was gracious. He slipped away when I walked up to them. He made excuses. His chowder needed seasoning or something. But Karen's eyes kind of trailed off after him, and the next time she was in town she called Kline, not me.

Talk about referred pain. At various times I've felt that event over my whole body. When I thought about it then, it was instant sinus trouble. Yesterday when I thought it, my knees ached. You can easily guess the other locations that have troubled me when I thought about the Moses and Karen combo.

I'm never resigned to these defeats, you know. I studied all the time. I worked out twice a week with a pro at the local tennis club—something I couldn't really afford then. Once in a while I sent Karen/Maggie a friendship card. She wasn't going to forget me. I wouldn't let her. And I watch every move Kline makes. Partly, I admit, it was out of tremendous admiration for a guy who could keep a streak going on so many levels all at once, and maybe I can learn something from him. But mainly I'm looking for the chink in the armor. Know your enemy, the guerillas say. I'm studying Moses Kline like I'm studying Merck's, the chemistry Bible, like Mao studied peasants.

Then one morning we were walking home together after a really trying night including a cocaine-crazed kid with a stab wound we couldn't settle down enough to work on, not for hours. The kid was really strong and very paranoid about doctors, and Kline and I were tired from trying to control him and from putting up with his psychotic tantrums.

"What else can we do?" Kline asked at one point.

"Defenestration," I said.

Kline smiled conspiratorily. "I'm just about ready for it," he said.

Ah, I thought. The man has limits.

We were approaching the intersection where we'd head our separate ways, and I was just about to ask Kline a loaded question about his relationship with Karen when we both saw in a flash of car lights a man down in the alley, a grimy bundle, flat on his back, face pale and gray-stubbled. Immediately we pulled him away from the wall and checked him out for any open wounds, airway obstruction, any sign of heartbeat, called for help and began CPR—all by the book, which book also says that once you begin CPR you can never stop until relieved. This guy stank of booze and vomit and his whiskers rasped my face, but I tried to put aside my disgust and listen to Kline counting away on his heart massage and then ventilate the guy on the right beats. The guy did feel a little warm, so we thought there was a chance.

I kept shouting at manual-prescribed times between breaths, but nobody responded. Kline pumped away until the sweat was running from his nose, and then we switched, making a smooth exchange, like a good double-play combination, or a fast-break pass into the key for an easy lay-up. Now Kline was the one breathing, shouting for help, and I pumped and counted.

The city is chockablock with people, but we were raising nobody with our cries. I was determined to pump the rest of the night away if necessary, but it's surprising how demanding the job became, how awkward the stance is, what muscles suddenly cry out for respite and to hell with the old drunk. So Kline and I switched again, again, again. I got into it—I mean, I got into it in my way. It couldn't be that long before the dawn and people began milling and paid attention to our shouts—hoarse shouts by now—but I was in no hurry because I was waiting to see how much Kline could take, and I thought, I'm going to beat him, I'm going to outlast him finally, and he's going to beg to quit.

And I saw how I was thinking: Kline was doing it to save the old man; I was doing it to beat Kline. We'd see which was the stronger medicine. I really wanted to see Kline faint with fatigue. The old boozer meant nothing to me. I was sure he was dead, past dead, beyond hoping for. And for what were we going to save him? More brown-bagging on grimy streets?

Kline doesn't have thoughts like this, I was sure of it. I thought: what's wrong with him?

Then Kline was counting in just a whisper, and his hair is hung over his face, he's gasping with fatigue (and I know perfectly well what he's feeling), and I'm the one, I say it first anyway: "Shall we stop?"

And Kline whispers, "Yeah. Let's stop."

We sit there on our knees, breathing hard, looking down at the gray-stubbled face we had been kissing for so long, the stare and the mocking grin, and I go crazy or something, I reach over and I wrap my arms around Kline and put my head on his shoulder and the little strength I have left, I'm hugging this man, and he hugs back.

"It'll happen again," he says, voice raw and cracking, "and we'll like it even less."

We let go of each other.

I draw my pistol—the metaphorical one. "Kline," I say, "I love you." Then I fire. "That's why I hate you."

I'm not sure he's heard me, but he's looking me straight in the eyes, lips tight. He fires back: "We can't fix everything."

I stand up first and I help him up, and we groan and brush off our knees and try to spit, and walk out of the alley together, looking for a telephone. Gunfighters in the street. The good citizens have apparently ducked for cover, and stayed there. You'd think we were alone on the planet. When we found the nearest phone, we discovered that neither of us had a goddamn quarter to make the call, and for some reason this caused us to laugh like idiots. And when the cowards emerged from their apartment buildings the first thing they saw that morning was Kline and me, grubby and drunk with fatigue, pounding the sides of a telephone booth and roaring out our defeated hearts.

Lawless in New York

Ms. Reinquist did not want to be falling in love with Professor Potter, but it was already happening, and after only two Manhattans. He was awful, really, in his damned light gray herringbone jacket and bow tie, the white hair at his temples closely shaved, his mustaches neat as a car salesman's, his rimless glasses and, yes, his poor bald pate, both reflecting the glum lights of the bar.

Everyone was drinking too much and talking too loudly, and of course they were making a spectacle of themselves as unsophisticated hicks in this elegant bar where Susan Sontag and Norman Mailer had no doubt insulted each other; where Max Perkins surely bought a drink for Thomas Wolfe and Bennett Cerf had counseled Katherine Anne Porter. Maybe Hemingway had slugged somebody here, and Dorothy Parker, of course, had left some poor fool's ego in bloody ribbons.

Ms. Reinquist squeezed her eyes shut a moment to get a grip on things, and then she gave up. Well, what of it, her paper had been a wonderful success and she deserved a little release of tension. The problem was with Potter. What was going on? She had barely noticed him around the department before and, as always, he was being very correct toward her as a colleague.

"Your paper has them buzzing," he had said immediately afterward. "Wonderful!"

Now she was having some startlingly pornographic thoughts about him. *He's a jogger*, she thought, *he's probably got a little stamina,* and then she was depressed: *My mind is going straight to the Devil.*

"You're looking so serious, Alice," Bob Sanders said to her. "Having second thoughts about your paper?"

She forced a smile. "I just realized how tired I am."

"Any offers to publish that thing?" Potter asked.

He *would* ask that, she thought. "Yes," she said. "What do you know about the *Massachusetts Review*?"

"It's published in Massachusetts," Sanders said.

Ms. Reinquist thought the remark gratuitous, but Sanders, with red hair and a neatly trimmed red beard, was young and could be forgiven. He had also been undergoing a series of job interviews, and after a full day of making those rounds anyone might become a little unhinged.

"Strictly neoabolitionist," Potter said. "If we published anything like it in Illinois, we'd be shot for a bunch of commies."

The fourth member of the party, Professor Silver, swiveled around in his wheelchair and grabbed Potter fiercely by the elbow with his mechanical hand. This device looked so terribly much like a coat hanger that in bad moments Ms. Reinquist imagined stashing Silver in a closet during one of her many parties as a kind of living silent valet. He had been a long-standing *provocateur* on any faculty committee she'd ever endured, and was once both ineptly and adequately described as a "paraplegic rakehell." Silver was not a paraplegic. That was the inept part of the description. He had had an accident of some kind, which no one ever talked about, a few years before Ms. Reinquist moved to Illinois. She imagined, though Potter was responding warmly to it, Silver's battery-powered grip must hurt terrifically.

"Did I hear the dread word spoken?" Silver asked.

"Unhand me, you Red Menace," Potter said.

"The Domino Theory lives," Silver said. "First we come to

New York to an MLA convention where we are contaminated with liberal Eastern ideas . . ."

"But," Potter said seriously, "isn't it true that you were originally from New Jersey?"

"Agh!" Silver cackled, releasing Potter and covering both his eyes with his mechanical forearm. "My secret is out. Next, my cell will be destroyed."

Ms. Reinquist grimaced. They were acting like schoolboys, Potter who was what?—forty-seven? forty-four?—and Silver who was probably the most unparaplegic rakehell linguistics professor in existence. They were building a special platform for him in the Gondolier Room so he could wheel in and baffle everyone in the profession, and here he was indulging in hackneyed old departmental stuff about Midwestern conservativism and anticommunism. No doubt about it: New York had them all on the defensive. Joseph McCarthy's border was contiguous with theirs; and after all, they were eight hundred miles closer to the shrines of the Ivy League now than they had ever been in Skibab, Illinois.

Alas, no one from Harvard or Columbia had offered her a job yet. Did Harvardians read the *Massachusetts Review*? she wondered. Did anybody? Of course, she thought glumly, Harvardians don't read at all. They were too busy writing. She'd love to have a job at Harvard, she admitted, among all those rich young men with hairy tennis legs.

"As for being contaminated by Eastern ideas," Bob Sanders continued, "did you ever hear of Berkeley?"

"Careful," Ms. Reinquist said, "that's my alma mater."

"*Mater!*" Silver said, cackling, eyebrows raised.

"Yes, *mater*," Reinquist said.

"Strange that a system so historically patriarchal as the university should be referred to in the feminine at last," Silver mused. "And if, as we like to say in the Faculty Senate, the university *is* its faculty, does that make us faculty members part of the great Soul Mother, too? Are we the Mother? And, if so, what are we mothering? Students? Knowledge?"

"Each other?" Potter asked.

Ms. Reinquist groaned. "Sophists!" she snapped.

"Sapphist!" Silver shot back.

"Thank you, but not quite," Ms. Reinquist said. "I don't deserve the compliment, actually."

"Ah? And why is that?" Silver asked, ladling out the innuendo, with even a mean edge to his voice.

"I don't write lyrics. Just prose."

Silver wagged his finger at her. "Oh you're a hard case. Tough, clever. You won't even admit to being heterosexual. Your paper, by the way, was excellent."

"Yes, wasn't it?" Potter interjected.

"I didn't think you'd honor me with your presence, Professor Silver. I'm astonished."

"Not half as astonished as I am," Silver said. "I mean, really, I expected to blow you out of the water. But I was impressed, I have to admit. A fresh approach. Irritating, of course, as all new ideas are, at first, but persuasive."

"New ideas irritate you?" Ms. Reinquist asked mildly.

"Every blasted one of them," Silver said. "Especially when they concern women or are put in the context of that ghastliest of all academic inventions, Women's Studies, whatever that is."

Why, you little squirt, Ms. Reinquist thought. Incongruously—or was it?—she wondered if he also had a mechanical penis. Potter pushed another Manhattan in her direction and she accepted it with a nod even though the idea of drinking any more made her heart sink. She had once been called a cheap drunk. But consider the source, she reminded herself, that colossal Berkeley mistake she was only too happy to forget.

"Well?" Silver challenged her.

"You don't expect me to dignify an intemperate, prejudiced, drunken remark like that, surely?"

"Oh, well . . ." Silver waved his glass and smiled. "I've been drinking."

"That's no excuse."

"No?" Potter said. "What will we ever do without the excuse of drunkenness? Alcohol is the national scapegoat."

"No more excuses," Ms. Reinquist said.

"Impossible!" Silver said. "No one can live like that. You've *got* to have some excuses."

"Show me the person who lives without excuses," Sanders said, "and I'll show you a robot."

Silver coughed and wiped his chin with the back of his real hand. "Excuses and lies. Whatever could the Good Lord have been thinking of to make such rhetorical twisteries a piece of our miserable existence?"

"Freedom of choice," Potter said. "You can't have freedom of choice if you have to tell the truth always."

"I think it's worse than that," Silver said. "I think we're required to live by lies."

Ms. Reinquist thought momentarily of Wonder Woman's Golden Lasso, which made even the most cunning of evildoers unable to prevaricate.

"Chauvinists," she said coolly. "Of course, God was a woman."

"Oh yes, I've seen that poster," Potter said. "I'm quite willing to accept the concept. That gives us males an excuse, finally, for all the abuse we've been taking lately. Let Her take the blame."

"How dare you?" Ms. Reinquist teased. "Everything is what it has to be. She is what She is."

"You know Kazantzakis's idea?" Sanders broke in. "He says

we improve our God by good actions and better thinking. That's wrestling with God for sure—to make Him, excuse me, Her better."

"I like that," Potter said, swirling his Scotch. "Very democratic, isn't it? It also improves the idea of wrestling with God immensely."

Led by Silver's speculations, the contingent plunged into a discussion of whether or not God, being possibly both male and female, should not also have a "hermaphroditic appellation." Just as Ms. Reinquist began to muse about what nice hands Professor Potter had, the conversation degenerated into an argument about whether or not grammatical gender had any necessary correlation to biological gender. Potter's observations on the habitual use of "man" in common parlance brought on a fit from Silver.

"Dead horse! Dead horse!" Silver slammed his glass on the table.

"It is not a dead horse," Ms. Reinquist said firmly, defending Potter. "Until the problem is solved, it will not go away. We think problems are solved just because we get tired of hearing about them."

"I know, I *know*," Silver said in a miserable tone. "I became an English teacher so I could read good books and dabble in poetry. I don't know the meaning of *macho*. And now, my God, me, who is lucky to have a nice family sexual encounter once a month—suddenly I'm some kind of villain because the language I love and study . . ."

"Oh, crap!" Ms. Reinquist said.

Sanders attempted to divert the discussion to Shakespeare's possible sexism, but by now the rifts in the Illinois contingent's social fabric, the lateness of the hour, and the effects of the alcohol deflated this attempt. Silver reminded everyone he was delivering a paper early in the morning and that he was also on the tenure committee, a remark directed particularly to Sanders.

"I'll be there," Sanders said, "hangover and all." He put his fingers to his temples. "Why do I do this to myself?"

"It's all this irresistible talk about gender and sex," Silver said. He raised his glass. "Here's to a hermaphroditic language."

"And good night!" Sanders took a rather long look at Ms. Reinquist before he left and she was startled at the idea he was expressing interest in her, sexual interest. How odd. She smiled politely, as if encountering a stranger in the elevator. She was lightly touched by his mood, but not much, she had to admit. Alcohol did not encourage subtleties, and she had had too much of both all day.

In a short while, Silver whirred off toward the main lounge of the hotel where, he said, he was going to do his damnedest to ram the editor of a journal who had returned one of his manuscripts with a snide comment or two. He described his planned approach in detail and claimed he was having some razorlike attachments made for the wheels of his machine just for occasions like this when he wanted to perform some James Bondish terror tactic or wreak revenge on unappreciative editors. Then, just before he left, he dumped his ice cubes in the ashtray and pocketed the glass.

"He's a madman," Potter said as soon as Silver was out of earshot. "Really. He was telling me today how he was going to use the stuff he's learned about computers—for his research?—to program his wheelchair. Someday, he vows, he'll only have to push a button or two and will be conveyed on journeys and errands without having to think about it at all. He'll nap, or read. He promises to keep up a regimen of such strict promptness and exactitude that he'll undermine the whole university."

"Really?"

"Well, just imagine if committees actually met on time and concluded business on schedule—or were forced to."

"We'll know how to vote if such a man runs for department chairman, of course."

"Against, clearly."

"Who could stand a robot for a leader?"

"We're awful," Potter said. "He's not a robot."

"We're just indulging his fantasy. That's not so bad, is it?" Ms. Reinquist knew she was betraying her weariness. If she weren't careful she would start babbling to this man. To keep things light, she asked Potter why he wore such awful clothes, "bow ties and things."

"Ah, I'm just an old hippie," Potter said, blushing a little and looking at himself.

"If you're a hippie, then I'm Joan of Arc."

"Quite a combo," he grinned. "I just wear the uniform of the profession of old. You see, I thought it was camp."

"It is that."

"But I'll change if you like."

"You'd take my opinion that seriously?"

"I don't want to be an old square, do I?"

"Square, maybe. But not so old."

"I suppose I've got fifteen years on you at least." He grimaced and then laughed. " 'April Inventory.' "

"Think of all the practice you've had."

"*Practice*?" Potter laughed softly. "I'd like to think I'm not practicing any more. I know what I can do, and can't do. There's only so much time."

"You're good at what you do." She said this in as matter-of-fact way as possible.

"At my age, I try to be realistic. In some respects that means I stay in my groove."

"No risks?"

"If you mean would I throw up everything and run off to medical school, the answer is 'no.' If you mean would I go bonkers over an overappreciative sophomore lass, the answer is also 'no,' but probably with regrets. What *do* you mean?"

"I don't really know," she said. "I'm asking for myself, too, I suppose. What's the big risk at the university anyway? Disapproval from the top? It's a silly thing to worry about, but I do."

"Really!" Potter said. "The dean, you know, he *likes* the way I dress. He doesn't see it as a joke. English professors are supposed to be . . . uh . . . can I say it? *Natty.*"

"God!"

"Really!"

"I haven't got a chance, do I? How will a 'modern young woman' ever achieve the natty look?"

Potter reassured her that her credentials and affirmative action pressure made her a good prospect to rise in the ranks, and quickly. He confided that the dean had mentioned her in conversations relating to possible promotions. And then he yawned and asked if they were going to have another drink.

"I'm afraid I can't," Ms. Reinquist said.

"Well, I'm afraid I can. I shouldn't, but I could."

"I take it you're not planning on jogging in the morning."

"In New York? I wouldn't know where to do it. Besides, did you ever jog with a hangover?"

"I've never jogged period." Ms. Reinquist regretted the tone of her voice. He'd think she was bored, and she wasn't really. She was suddenly weary, and awfully sad. As usual, nothing was going to happen. It was all right to spend time like this if it were a prelude to something, or if it clarified relationships, even if it only expressed friendly feelings. But this was fading out into nothing, and she hated the waste. Must every day dissolve into the great Blah? Wasn't this supposed to be Fun City?

Potter attempted to return to the topic of Ms. Reinquist's paper, but she put him off.

Potter waved his glass. "Just trying to carry on."

"Very valiant of you, considering the company."

"You're worn out?"

"Professor Potter . . ." Ms. Reinquist's heart accelerated momentarily. "I hope you won't think me too awfully forward or too kinkily weird if I tell you I am not only drunk but in the grip of the Golden Lasso and more than anything else I have been thinking all evening about having your head between my breasts."

Potter's eyes seemed to go out of focus for a moment and she was afraid he would laugh, or insult her, and she almost bolted. What *had* she done?

"My dear," he replied sadly, and in a mode as formal as her own, "I would jump at the chance."

Ms. Reinquist felt a wave of embarrassment, then relief, and actually began to wake up. She felt redeemed. Suddenly they both began to laugh, and reached for each other, clumsily entwining their arms.

"My God," she said. "This is the most lawless thing I've ever done."

The time had been blurry and pleasant. Was it better than masturbation? Yes, a dozen times. He had stamina, he was kind, quiet and grateful. Better than religion? Yes, temporarily at least. And he had not stayed all night so the fellows he was rooming with would not have too much to speculate about. They might slip up in front of Potter's wife and neither of them wanted that. To be gone all night would be too much for Skibab society, even the university liberals. Besides, it was a relief to be alone afterwards, to lounge in the shower and not be embarrassed by how she looked in the morning and the awful preparations she was going through to get ready for Silver's lecture. Her head ached brutally and she was not sure she could even endure a breakfast now, though they all agreed to meet for one—in twenty minutes? She'd never make it in twenty minutes, not without an act of heroism, or a miracle.

In between the peals of pain in her head, she thought of how nicely Potter's hands had held her rump as she lay on top of him. That was sustenance. That gave her the energy she needed to put herself in motion at last.

She knew when she came into the hallway she was wearing a bluish pallor, but that was probably going to be the general aura of the Illinois contingent this morning, she guessed. She locked her door and turned toward the elevator where she saw young Bob Sanders, sober and ruddy, and even natty—the bastard. He had been holding the elbow of a woman Ms. Reinquist did not know, but dropped his hand swiftly when he saw her, and said something to her between his teeth. The woman wore a purple leotard top which was dotted with the nipples of her breasts; her hair was dyed deep black—or perhaps it was a wig. She wore a short skirt and when she shifted her weight from one leg to the other Ms. Reinquist was sure she heard a hiss of nylon. In spite of herself, she blushed. She was embarrassed for Sanders, but decided she would be politely oblivious, urbane as possible. This was New York. They were adults.

Against her hopes, Sanders held the elevator door for her and she was forced to come into the presence of the woman he had spent the night with. The perfumy presence almost made her ill; the snick-snacking of her gum chewing was like the ticking of a clock.

"Good morning, Ms. Reinquist."

"How are you, Sanders?"

He didn't answer and looked at the floor as the elevator rapidly dropped.

"Well?" the woman said. "What about it?"

Sanders held up a finger. "Just a minute," he said.

Ms. Reinquist was glad at least Bob hadn't tried to lie, or to make pleasantries. Was he going to pay her, though? Had they been dickering about a price? The thought made her nauseous. When the doors opened she bolted for the women's room where she splashed her face with cold water, took about thirty deep breaths, and delivered a relieving belch that would have shocked King John, say, or an Arab prince. She congratulated herself on the force of it, suddenly felt better, and went in to breakfast with a more authoritative air than she would have thought possible only moments before.

The mood around the breakfast table was fairly grim, as they had all predicted it would be, given the intensity of last night's merrymaking. Potter seemed a little dazed, and it was awkwardly apparent how determined he was to pay just the right amount of attention to her. On her part, Ms. Reinquist was afraid she would show how deeply in love she was, and her resentment of that stupid fact. Damn it! She didn't want to be in love with a married man. Or a colleague. Or a friend of friends. She had broken all her rules, and consequently found herself on the periphery of a miasmal swamp.

Sanders sulked. What's the matter? she wanted to ask him. Did you get a bad deal? Was he actually ashamed she had found him out?

Silver, for all his reputation, was plainly nervous about his lecture. He kept leafing through the pages on his lap and complaining how unfinished the piece was because of computer jinxes, time limits, undependable graduate assistants, and . . . Ms. Reinquist tuned out. The orange juice was wonderful, but she left half her scrambled eggs. Potter had an apple Danish and was very, very self-conscious about eating it. She tried not to watch his teeth sink into the sugar frosting again and again.

"Did you ram your editor last night?" she asked Silver.

"Shhhhh!" He looked around wildly. "It was supposed to be an accident. You'll get me hung for malice aforethought."

"Forgive me."

"Of course. But between us—by his limp you shall know him." He smiled devilishly and slapped his papers. "You wait. He'll come begging for this one."

They left together in a clump and, with Silver's wheelchair taking up half the space, commandeered an entire elevator for themselves. Ms. Reinquist and Potter were crushed together in a rear corner. Furtively he stroked her thigh, but she pulled his hand away. The elevator rose too rapidly. *Or am I sinking?* she thought. *I'm not like that. There's got to be a difference.* She felt she was floating for a moment as the elevator slowed.

Silver whirred ahead of them, but his chair stopped suddenly in the doorway and the doors began to close again. Sanders batted them open.

"What the hell," Silver muttered. "On, you huskies!"

"It's O.K., you're just caught here where the elevator's not level with the floor." Potter raised the back of the chair by the handles and pushed it gently forward. The papers slid out of Silver's lap and fluttered like pigeons into the hallway.

"Back! Back!" Silver ordered.

Potter obeyed, and then he and Sanders stepped out to retrieve the papers Silver had dropped. The doors snarled shut and the elevator began to drop before Ms. Reinquist could reach the hold button.

"This isn't going to be my day," Silver said.

"It is a nuisance," Ms. Reinquist said, pressing buttons on the elevator panel. "But only a nuisance."

"Life is a nuisance," Silver said. "Ninety percent of it."

"Pessimist," she scolded.

"For a man in a wheelchair, I'd say that was a generous assessment of the case."

"I *don't* feel sorry for you, you know."

"I know. I love you for it. It's people like you who keep me from trying to kill myself again."

"That's a terrible thing to say." Ms. Reinquist almost shouted. "Even as a joke."

"I'm not joking," Silver said. "Last time I tried it with a car. Hence, this machinery." He waved his mechanical arm.

"Why do you think I'm interested?" Ms. Reinquist hissed. "This is hell!"

"Heaven!" Silver laughed. "I can't think of anybody I'd rather be stuck in an elevator with."

"Goddamn you," she said. She held her hands over her eyes and started to weep. *I'm not like that,* she thought. She hated him. She hated Potter, too. She hated everything.

"Save your tears for somebody who needs them," Silver said as the doors opened again. "I scorn your pity."

"We thought we lost you there," Potter laughed. "Here's your paper. We even had time to collate."

"Thank you kindly," Silver said.

Potter held out his hand for Ms. Reinquist and from the look on his face she could tell that he saw she had been crying. No doubt her mascara was wrecked. Perhaps she should not be seen in the lecture hall with her face all streaked. Someone from Harvard might see her, or City College. Maybe she should leave New York at once.

"I'm sorry," she said to no one in particular, sucking in her grief and becoming fierce and professional once more. "It won't happen again."

New Line

Walter is at the Cape Cod Canal, jigging, five-thirty in the morning. His left arm is killing him, thanks to Benoit's punches from the night before, and he has a hangover that makes the usually hard work of jigging even harder. He wishes he could quit drinking. The jig comes up out of the driving current covered with eelgrass and a spongy brown seaweed, which is O.K., shows that the jig has been on the bottom, where the fish are when the fish are there at all.

A good bass is worth money now. Right now the wholesale price is two-fifty a pound, whole, a forty-pounder means a hundred bucks. The five-ounce jig is yellow, has a skirt of bucktail, and a piece of red pork rind trails from the single hook. Walter strips the jig of seaweed, then casts it up current, his shoulder aching with the stress of the effort, waits for the lure to drift to the bottom, then retrieves it, alternating quick upward bursts and a slow sinking down, to imitate the motions of a squid. Walter is going at it hard this morning, trying to sweat out the booze.

When the fish hits, Walter knows it is a good one, and a bass, because it stops the line dead and then just lays low for a moment. The fish takes in the new reality slowly, has no strategy. A few seconds later, it swings into the current and shakes its head once or twice, and then, more violently, takes line. Walter cranks but drops the rod tip so that he will be able to pump the fish up or reel quickly if it decides to come towards him. But so far the fish has not panicked and is loafing on the bottom, using the current to tug at the odd pressure trying to turn it, and take it up. Walter wonders if the fish can even remotely understand its problem, what has suddenly intruded into its life.

Walter's own problems are knots, all the things that can go wrong. The fish could cruise close to the canal walls, drag the line over mussel beds. Walter is pretty sure of his knots, though, and always takes pains with them, tests them, jams them tight using pliers and special gloves. But there is always something. The snap could be pulled open, and the damned line, really the damned line should have been changed and it might be nicked and only yesterday morning he had been cranking in bluefish and the line was stretched and probably even nicked. The line whistles now from the tension of fish and current and because the fingers of the wind pluck it like a harpist—another sign of a good fish, that siren whistling of the line.

Walter tries to budge the fish, to see if he can pry it up from the bottom and away from all the mussel beds and junk and wrack down there, ghost lobster traps, the big, waxy brown arms of kelp that could snarl the line if the fish drops down and into such a bed. For reply, the fish takes line in short bursts, the drag squealing each time.

And then is gone. The line parts, not with any sharp ping or crack but as if it had melted, a sure sign it has been nicked somewhere. Walter howls in anger as he reels in the proof of the fish's escape, feeling nothing at all. Goddamn the goddamned bluefish, worthless bastards, sharp teeth and all! He swears and bitches and blames himself because he had been in the Red Top Tackle Shop only yesterday and had thought then he should take the twenty minutes to have new line put on the reel, and didn't because . . . Ah, shit, he thinks, because I didn't want to spend the five or six bucks because then I'd be out of drinkin' money. The memory of the weight of the fish, its solidity, irritates him, brings home the finale of his loss. He swears, rummages in his tackle bag, rerigs, and is soon fishing again. I'm going to quit, he says. That's it. I'm through drinkin'. Wouldna had that fight. Woulda had new line. And that fish would be slappin' tail right here at my feet.

That afternoon, about four-thirty, Walter is seated in the usual place, and he orders the usual drink. When it is served, the bartender, Furtado, says, "You know the cops are lookin' for you?"

"What?" Walter says. "Christ, no. Why?"

"They was in here earlier, askin' for you."

"Jesus Christ," Walter says, "Who's 'they'?"

"The Bobbsey Twins," Furtado says. "Clark and Donati."

"But why?"

Furtado shrugs, raises his thick eyebrows, pouts. "Maybe Benoit filed charges. How do I know what you been up to? Maybe you aren't keepin' up child support. Maybe you didn't pay a parkin' ticket."

"*What!*" Walter says, profoundly irritated now. "You think Benoit would file over a lousy fistfight?"

"You hurt him pretty bad," Furtado says.

"Well, he hurt me, too." Walter lifts his left shoulder in illustration. It really hurts still.

"You didn't have to keep on him like that," Furtado says, staring past Walter, then dropping his gaze when he adds: "But that's the type of guy Benoit is. Any excuse, he'll run to the cops."

Walter takes a sip of his drink, feeling with it a jolt of fear: *I won't be able to stop now.* "Goddamn that Benoit," he says. "He's been a total pain in the ass from the first day I met him."

"He says the same thing about you."

"I wish I'd just went ahead and killed the bastard."

Furtado leans down on the bar and looks directly into Walter's eyes. "If I were you, I wouldn't say nothin' like that. Not out loud, not in a public place. Somebody might think you meant it. Y' hear me?"

Walter nods, takes Furtado's advice and keeps his mouth shut. But he thinks: I do mean it. He curses Benoit silently as he sings also the familiar litany of Benoit's crimes, beginning with moving in with Judy and thereby crushing any hopes of Walter's reconciliation with his ex-wife, but not really even ex-, not just yet. Then the latest bullshit, volunteering some unflattering opinions about Walter to Captain Frost and costing him that job. That had been too much. That's when he had decided to teach Benoit a lesson, and now, goddamn it, he had turned around and gone running to the cops. Walter finishes his drinks and thinks, Maybe I *should* just kill him. Knock his ass down the canal rocks, throw him in the water. Shove him into the train some night when it comes slammin' through there. He's glued to me like a fuckin' lamprey or something, sucking out my blood. I got a right to be left alone. What's he think? He's God?

Walter has had two more drinks when the Bobbsey Twins walk in. Walter sees them approaching in the mirror, but doesn't turn around, just sits and drinks like a peaceable citizen until Clark is on one side and Donati on the other. Clark is tall and Irish with pale blue eyes; Donati is shorter with a Burt Reynolds kind of mustache and really hard, really spooky black eyes. Walter had been to high school with Clark, who is older than Donati by a good ten years.

Clark speaks. "Got a summons for you, Walter."

"Heard you was lookin' for me," Walter says. "What's the beef?"

"Beef?" Clark chuckles. "You been watchin' too many

movies. John Benoit filed this complaint against you for assault and battery. You're to appear in court October first."

Walter accepts the summons, rolls it up and stuffs it into his shirt pocket. He continues to drink and to regard the officers in the mirror, where they appear to him to be a little underwater. The illusion amuses Walter a little. Donati is chewing gum and looking frightened. Clark looks as if at any moment he might break into a yawn.

"So how's the family?" Walter says.

Clark smiles. "Show up, Walt. You could get thirty days. You could get thirty more for contempt."

"Thanks for the advice," Walter says.

Clark surveys the empty bar, then asks, "How's the fishin'? You making out all right?"

"Dropped a big one this morning," Walter says. He turns on the stool now and looks into Donati's face. "You do any fishin', do you, Offi-suh Donati?"

"No," Donati says. He chews on, nervous.

"Don't know what people do down here if they don't fish," Walter says.

"We work," Donati says, a little aggressively.

Furtado comes down the bar and greets the policemen. "You guys want some coffee?"

"We're on duty," Clark says.

Donati zips up his jacket. "I'm going out to the car," he says.

"Then I'll just have a coffee," Clark says. Over his shoulder he calls to Donati, "Call me if there's any mayhem."

"Like last night, you mean?" Walter says, and everyone laughs.

"You want any official bourbon in that coffee, Johnny?" Furtado slaps his hand on the bar.

"Yeah, sure." Clark takes off his hat and drops it in front of him. "Only hold the coffee, will you?"

"Just the way you like it." Furtado serves the policeman

a double bourbon in a coffee cup. "The kid's drivin' today, I take it."

"He gravels my ass sometimes," Clark says and smiles a weary smile. "But I trust him."

Walter drinks and watches his former schoolmate in the mirror. He can't believe it. Twenty years later and the heroes of gridiron and sandlot are still mucking around the hometown, going nowhere, pissing time away in a stupid joint.

"So, Walter, off the record," Clark says, "it's not my place to advise you on anything . . ."

"So don't," Walter says.

"So stay the hell away from John Benoit and get a good lawyer."

"I can't afford a lawyer."

"Get one anyway," Clark says.

"I can't afford a lawyer," Walter says, "because Benoit has been interferin' with every attempt I make to find a job that might pay for one. He's been tellin' lies about me all over town. You know what he told Captain Frost? About me?"

"I don't want to know," Clark says.

"He said I sexually abused my daughter." Walter spits. "That's what he's been sayin'."

"Don't punch him," Clark says. "Sue him. And look, that could come up. You need a good lawyer to handle that kind of crap. That's what I'm tryin' to tell you."

"You think it'll come up?" Walter trembles with a little rush of fear, shakes it off.

"I don't know what'll come up," Clark says.

"Suppose some asshole said that about you?" Walter demands. "Come on, Johnny. You'd sue him? You want everybody in town to be readin' that in the paper? How'd that go over down at headquarters?"

"I know how you feel," Clark says.

"You know how I feel but you sure as shit aren't answering my question, either," he says. "Of course Benoit wouldn't have the guts to say that about an armed man."

"Get a lawyer," Clark repeats. He slaps the coffee cup into his saucer, dons his hat, thanks Furtado and saunters out, gun riding his hip.

He looks O.K., Walter decides. Not in bad shape at all. Under that hat the bald spot doesn't show and he looks fine. If he doesn't get shot or run over, he might last a while. Must be all the walkin' he does, rattlin' doorknobs. Oh I don't know how to account for it, account for anything.

Furtado nods toward the door. "Damn nice fella."

"Donati's an eerie one, though," Walter offers.

"Ah." Furtado waves in disgust. "He's just too damned straight arrow. I think he's more afraid of losing his job than anything else."

"Well, you were right," Walter says. "Benoit ain't satisfied to libel me all over and prevent my workin'. He's got to see me in jail."

Furtado doesn't respond. He places one foot on a beer keg and looks out the window. After a moment he says, "You said you dropped a big one this morning. Where was that?"

Walter laughs and shakes his head. "That's right," he says. "That's what everybody really wants to know, ain't it? And while I'm rottin' down there in Barnstable jail during the prime fishin' time, you'll all be lined up along the canal bangin' the big ones and havin' a great old time. Won't you, Billy boy? Never mind Walter Frazier's down in the friggin' slammer slurpin' bean and potato soup. You want to borrow my rods, too, long as I won't be usin' 'em? Is that right?"

Furtado continues looking out the window, but a look of disgust crosses his face and unconsciously his lip curls. "Walter," he says, "you got a funny attitude. Sometimes you talk like a real loser. What are you gonna do? Just sit there and get smashed and let it all wash over you? Or take Johnny's advice? You know, he didn't have to tell you nothin'. You know that?"

"Oh, thanks." Walter looks in the mirror and wonders, Why the hell is everybody on my case right now? What did I do to deserve all this crap? I'm fishin', I'm mindin' my own business, and everything sinks, everything just kinda dissolves, or like somebody has held my head under water, under water too long. And I wake up and there's all this . . . *crap.*

"You get it on the jig?" Furtado asks now.

"That's right."

"What color?"

"White," Walter says. "White pork rind, too."

"No kidding? Right after the tide turned or later?"

"Two hours after," Walter says.

"How big?"

"How do I know how big? I didn't see it. Bluefish had my line all nicked. Poof! Away she went."

"Yeah, but what do you figure, based on the pull?"

"Fifty at least," Walter says.

"That big, huh?"

"Maybe it was a thirty that swallowed rocks. It's just a guess. But she hugged that bottom pretty tight and she lay right there, smart as a bitch."

"You'd know," Furtado says. "You've seen enough of them to know."

"That's right." The booze has begun to take hold, to make Walter a little less afraid. He feels a little sleepy, slumps on the stool to take the pressure off his left arm. "Goddamned bluefish," he says. "We'll never get the bass like we used to, not until the blues are weeded out." He wants to continue his complaint but cannot find the energy and Furtado seems lost in his own thoughts. He takes the summons out of his pocket and holds it between his legs, out of Furtado's sight, begins tearing it into smaller and smaller pieces, lets them float down into the sawdust on the floor. Goddamn it, he thinks, there'd be this chain. I'd say Benoit lied. They'd check it out. They'd call in Susan and they'd call in Judy. And she might say it. My own kid telling them in court. She might. All the pressure on her, all the pressure of their hate for me. She might say it.

I could try Florida. A couple of good fish like this morning and I'm out of here. I'll bang a jewfish off the bridge down there, something like that. I'll catch somethin' keep me goin'. Mako. Somethin' big. Canal ain't the only place to fish. Striper ain't the only fish God ever made.

The Connoisseur

Money is so stupid, yet utterly plastic, like paint. We try to invent new laws for it when there are none. Believe me, this is the key to success.

I used to think of money as a river on which you skillfully managed your kayak, being careful not to be swamped, or beached, always riding high and gracefully. That was in the days when it was convenient to believe I was in control of things, and events, and myself, that I became rich out of some inherent superiority, some glory of my own.

Because it fit the flow of money in my life, it made sense to me and was a pleasure to become a collector. Chinese vases and ceramics, Midwestern weavings and rugs: these were my first appropriations. I made some adept purchases and cluttered my house with these lovely, immaculate things. Then I became tainted, for history began to interest me, and I bought fragments of ancient junk, scraps of pottery, corners of royal shopping lists or inventories with the letters smudged and sanded down by time. What a wonderful Romantic melancholy I would feel in a room full of these shards: "Look on my works, ye Mighty, and despair!"

I could not go far enough back or deep enough down. The collector's hobby transformed into a genuine passion for digging out what time had collected in the earth. I hired people to dig for me, and told them where to go, though in fact some of the books these intelligent workers have written for me will say only that I supported their research. A trifle! For a long time I could only explain myself and these expenses by thinking that these pieces of historical junk had a high dollar value as well as some evidence for making up complicated theories about the people who went before us—permit me to be facetious—on a planet without oil wells and computers. Our idea of necessities, I think, is truly impoverished.

If it could have been foreseen how much and in what forms our generation would worship the pressurized gore of old fern forests, precautions might have been taken to burn it, or eat it all. But the dinosaur had a small brain. The maddest, most hashish-crazed, berry-drunk, food-poisoned dervish could not have envisioned the uses to which their dying world would be put. Even Ezekiel had no concept of rush hour. Even Newton would gasp at a night flight over Chicago.

These things, too, I began to accumulate: cuneiform tablets, sarcophagi, artifacts of the dead. And manuscripts passed down in time. Tomb-robbing, pure and simple. Robbing the dead. Was it so macabre of me to sense some string tied between my own heart and those which had beat long ago? These dusty, cracking lines of words: one, from Tibet, an expert informed me, told the story of how the gods, through a shower of their holy urinations, brought joy to all living beings and fertility to earth. In such regard were these immortals held, he went on, their very waste was considered magical. Also, he chuckled, their conception of the deity was limited by what the proto-Hindus knew humankind to be: eaters, pissers, shitters, copulators. This paradox of the divine as both magical and base amused us. What did we know? We were smug. Our gods wore diapers. We filled our museums with amusing anecdotes of primitive belief, dead legends, crumbled religions, while our own gods chuckled beside us.

There was so much to be exploited in Nepalese and Tibetan

lore that a group of us arranged a summer expedition—at a time, it turned out, when Katmandu had become a destination for experience-crazed youth, the longhairs of that era. They offended everyone by smoking *ganja* in the temples, by going barefoot (the bottoms of the feet are considered obscene there) and by walking clockwise, against the flow of bodies, around sacred buildings—those with the sharply curved roofs and the edgy eyes of Buddha peering out from the turrets. Of course they were to some degree innocent, unaware of the customs, but also they were ignorant, and even more unforgivably, simply unobservant.

We were not much interested in the city in any case or in what we were told were the all-night sessions of drugs, music, and lovemaking on the starving paradises of the beaches farther south. Instead, we packed with mules and yaks into the Himalayan foothills, following a trail said to have been taken by a Tibetan holy man who founded the seven monasteries we hoped to visit. We were accompanied by local guides and government aides—these now being Chinese, of course, since the Dalai Lama had fled some years before—and so made an official sort of progress and were introduced to some appropriately second-rate treasures which we bought more out of a sense of duty than any appreciation for their beauty or value.

The countryside—such a term is utterly inadequate—was stupendous. The craggy heights of the Himalayas swept over and around us like giant teeth, and though we steadily climbed into thinner and thinner air, and moved more and more slowly, our feet never left soft, rolling, grassy earth, like a perpetual meadow rising into the clouds. This alone, for the moment, saved the journey from becoming little more than a government-sponsored hike to elevated curio shops, a trek through dirty little towns full of hostile dogs and begging (or thieving) children.

One afternoon, nearing the fifth monastery, we realized we had achieved a near-perfect exhaustion (we foreigners, that is, and not our guides, our *sherpas*) and halted the train for a long afternoon's rest. Though it was cold, I slept in the grass away from the animals and the others, occasionally opening my eyes to a sky as blue as the enamel in a cloisonné vase. I was tired of haggling with the others and of the propaganda of our government sponsors and so, when I awoke, I slipped away down a path through the tall grass in search of a place to be alone for a while.

I had not gone far when, to my irritation, I saw ahead a young, obviously Western youth squatting by the trail. He seemed to have just finished relieving himself and carefully held up the hem of his robe as he moved back onto the path. When I came closer I could see his beard was thin, and blonde, his feet were obscenely bare with toenails broken and toes bruised, and his eyes were dark with abuse and personal negligence. I was in no mood for conversation, especially not with an American of this sort, and so walked past him with a perfunctory nod. This must have amused him, for he began to laugh. I looked back, angry, and saw that his upper lip was pulled back over his teeth in an animal-like snarl.

"Where do you think you are?" he laughed. "New York?"

"Go to hell," I said.

He threw up his hands in disgust and amazement. "Such a sick heart. Why don't you lose it here?" He danced clumsily off the path, obviously insane, and sang *Chicago, Chicago, that toddlin' town.*

"Do you want help?" I called.

"Do you?" he shot back.

"We can get you to a doctor."

"Oh boy," he said.

"Take my advice," I said. "Just over the rise is a group of

people who will look after you. We could have you on a plane in two days."

"You take my advice," he replied, apparently unable to stifle his laughter. "Don't let anybody piss in your yogurt." Then he tumbled recklessly down the slope, as if there were not a stone or a snake on the whole hillside, as if his feet were indestructible.

I was stunned. After a moment, I broke into a laugh, too, at the absurdity of the whole encounter. I wanted to shout the man back, but he was already too far away, head and shoulders bobbing above the grass. All the futile questions that came to mind!

I realized that of course I had been rude, that the young indigent had been right about my state of mind. Perhaps it was the mountain air—or perhaps exhaustion was to blame. In any case I sat in the slope of that glorious meadow and began to worry about my hostility and frustration, a kind of meanness I had become habituated to lugging around, as if it were normal and necessary. As most people would have done in such a moment of self-scrutiny, I found myself wanting in all but material success. What did I really know about life or other people? I asked myself. I knew a great deal about things, certainly; I knew a great deal also about the uses of money. That is, it occurred to me, I knew how to play Monopoly. I knew how to stay out of jail, charge rent, build hotels, and pass Go. In the financial world, I had become quite clever at passing Go, and at this point did not even have to be present to play the game, but could play it by proxy. Playing by proxy: that was how I did everything now, arranged everything now. Almost.

This realization was utterly wearying. I pulled grass out of the ground in fistfuls and threw it into the wind. The peaks of the Himalayas thundered like railroad cars in a dream. There was a village about three miles away. On higher slopes we had seen the cluster of saffron-yellow buildings in the distance and debated whether to pass through, but the government aides insisted the places were too far out of the way and entirely too ordinary to bother with. The path I had been following surely led to one such town, and I decided to follow it on my own, let the rest hang and be bothered—they had plenty of food and might enjoy the chance to sneak off with each other in the grass. Even on this more athletic, quasispiritual trip, we had accumulated a great deal of sleeping-bag lore, and I could not see what harm a little more sexual intrigue could do at this point. Battles had been fought, lines drawn, conquests made. I was tired of it.

As I was about to leave, one of the *sherpas* from our caravan appeared and in his polyglot broken-English, broken-French, broken-Chinese urged me to rejoin the group. Some sort of argument had broken out which called for a decision on my part, nothing of substance really, but more a matter of everyone's fatigue and jealousy and impatience and probably even just their smelly shirts and itchy underwear that found its focus on a trivial item of debate such as whether or not we were going to send for more supplies (via helicopter) or bypass one of the monasteries in order to meet our well-named deadlines.

The *sherpa*, who was not involved in the debate, did not help to clarify the problem. He was more inclined to sit in the deep grass and smoke *ganja* and observe the wool-like clouds packing together over the mountaintops. I envied his objectivity and for a moment I imagined myself in his shoes, showing a bunch of clumsy, wrangling foreigners through the mountains and the sanctuaries that had been exclusively his and those of his countrymen for so many years—not to mention "the Home of God." And yet he did not seem nasty or cruel towards us; he simply waited for us to make up our minds, and was meanwhile content to lay back with his head on the belly of a donkey and gaze at the clouds and the mountains. He must have had political opinions, family worries, ideas about himself and about us, but nevertheless appeared always patient, cheerful, and damnably tireless.

A man like this, I thought, would have been fired in my corporation for being too suspect, as having no drive, or will. Here, of course, he was as much a part of the place as the grass, and imagining him in a suit and tie was all but impossible. What we looked for in a young executive was commitment, as we named it, meaning that greed became his or her priority. Creative greed. Perhaps the *sherpa* could drive a hard bargain in the marketplace or would sell his own mother firewood at an extravagant price. Who was I to say he was blessed with peace? It just seemed likely that if you asked him for something, he would give it away. Was there anything in particular he would miss? I wondered. What would cause him grief to surrender or part with? His prayer wheel? His *ganja?* His mule?

The answer was simple: the Himalayas. Take away his mountains and he would die, he would be astounded and lost. And this would be an easy thing to do, in a sense: suppose we kidnapped him to Chicago and turned him loose in the streets? His frame of reference would be shattered, his peace (and his unintentional arrogance) destroyed. It would be tantamount to murder.

I returned to camp and played judge. After all these years, I don't even remember what the hubbub was about, something to do with one of the treasures we had accumulated, a gilt scroll, a multiple prayer wheel, an ancient printing block (which I think the *sherpas* would have valued more as firewood than holy relic), or some assignment of duties. Our weariness had thrown everything out of proportion, and since I was myself impatient to the point of shouting, I made some ultimatums, demoted one fellow and later, in the privacy of my tent, made unnecessary demands of a young woman who attracted me and who had been flirtatious. I did everything, that is, to make my sick heart worse, I played the master. So I woke early with only my *sherpa* to realize it and watch me wander off, toward that village I had seen in the distance the day before. It was still dark, the high peaks interfering with the sun. And cold. The stars rang like bells overhead. The *sherpa* watched a while, then dropped back to sleep.

I should have remembered that these mountain villagers let their dogs roam at night. As soon as I came onto the main street—the sun was just staining the sky with red embers—I was surrounded by four mastiffs whose bared fangs and insane, ceaseless barking made it easy for me to imagine myself torn to shreds and left, say, like a smashed squirrel on the highway. I was in a sweat of terror which was not relieved when a few men in the town sleepily appraised the ruckus and apparently found it appropriate and right. To my anger and increased terror, they made no move to whistle off the dogs, not until I called to them in a beseeching and exasperated voice; and even so they moved with a suspicion and a reluctance that made me think they would have believed it better, or more natural, for the dogs to rend me like a deer, my eyes wide with that astonishment and pain common to all things killed in the wild.

Once the dogs were driven off, chained, and I was apparently safe, I wanted to rail. Was I among men who would allow such a thing to happen, who could let another be ripped apart by dogs? But I smothered my outrage with mock gratitude and made every sign I could of being humble and harmless—which was no great effort when I saw the dogs thrashing against their chains.

What a pathetic village. Mud, ruts in the road, dogs, always the damned dogs, because people are afraid of each other, and dogs hear better, see better, smell better—vastly—give advance warning, make a thief or a killer think twice. Crime even here, I supposed, though of what kind I could only guess. No whores drawing crowds of conventioneers, obviously, but something more subtle. An area with a few wooden stalls suggested a marketplace, and this interested me. Things were made here, surely, demand was realized, people schemed to create and fulfill a want, a need. I had no idea what I could find in this place, having more than enough treasures already to burden our animals with, and it seemed unlikely I would find anything to carry away, and be happy with the exchange. Inevitably I wondered what I could bring to this town that they would want, and spend their meager resources for.

I thought the dogs had assessed me at a glance: thief and exploiter. Certainly they would have been kinder to a man carrying food or firewood or cloth.

The town had something for me I would not have anticipated, could not have anticipated, thinking in these terms. They had mushrooms. And I paid something unexpected and dear for them as well: my past.

There was no place to go in this village, nothing to see, not even, as far as I could assess, a public place, a tearoom. In these villages, you have to know where to go, no signs direct you, for it is assumed that if you do not know, then you have no business there. Strangers are not expected and not encouraged to linger. The town's history was full of thieves and warlords —another reason for the damned dogs—invaders, kidnappers of women. And yet I had no desire to return to the wrangles in my camp and was content to eavesdrop and spy a while longer. Some sheep and a lone yak scrounged in a ruined field nearby. Now and then the yak would lift its heavy head and let out a raw bellow that was the perfect note, a sympathetic vibration with whatever part of me it is we call the heart, or soul. If I had been alone on a mountainside, I would have answered that bellow in kind.

Someone's cooking fire triggered my own hunger. I had never fasted or, for that matter, ever even dieted seriously. Perhaps I had missed a meal or two while traveling or engaged in some sport or entertaining diversion. It was a little astonishing to think that in a land where people were climbing to the tops of trees to procure fodder for their animals, eating grasshoppers, and making a tea of bark (and pepper, when they could get it), I would expect to have my belly filled at the usual times and, in fact, had arranged for that to happen as always, not only for myself but for the whole entourage. Surely the people at my camp were already cooking their morning meat and rice, preparing their coffee and bread. I wondered if I had missed five meals in my entire lifetime and marveled that by the inevitable trail of my ancestry and the accidents of history I would emerge on the planet as a person who had consumed, so I calculated, about 43,800 consecutive meals. And wanted another!

To distract myself, I hiked up a spare lane into some hills where boulders and some ragged blue rocks broke through the soil. There was a cluster of trees here that ran across a ridge and then spread out like a hand in a lower-lying area. Like all the trees remaining in this ravaged country, they had been pruned almost to their tops and were scraggly and broken. I sat down in this grove at a point where I could observe the activity in the village below and also enjoy the sun a little. My hunger continued to gnaw.

My daydreaming was interrupted by the sound of children laughing and arguing and some surly commands from their mothers. I think I surprised them when they came over the ridge, and though they were curious, they did not speak to me. All wore several layers of thick skirts, jolly vests, cloth belts, and woolen caps with large flaps over the ears. Evidently they had been foraging, for the women carried small bundles of sticks across their backs, and the children carried little leather bags with a small quantity of mushrooms in them, some brown and wrinkled as bark (a kind of morel, I would learn later) and a few only that were large and bright red, dusted with white flakes like some confection—the fly agaric, which has so many names and such a hidden history. How innocent my perception then! The mushroom was pretty and looked sweet. This is how the Devil and God do their work, and children poison themselves: surely such a plant is candy.

I knew better than to make any sort of approach to the women, curious as I was about them, not just because of the inevitable language barrier, but out of respect for their customs. But as an older woman was following the clump of mothers and children, I appealed to her and indicated my hunger, so I hoped, by pointing to the mushrooms she so carefully carried in her apron. What sense she made of my gestures I don't know, but her reply was both quick and harsh and let me know I was on dangerous turf with her. I should keep my distance, she seemed to say, but if I followed and behaved myself, perhaps something could be done for me. I stood and bowed and followed her into the village like a servant, or a man under arrest.

She led me into the center of a cluster of buildings where, as in all these villages from Africa to northern Japan, there was a well, surely as important as a gathering place for the women (and sometimes unmarried men) as for the water it provided. The old woman made it clear I was to sit on a bench in the corner of this well-trampled lot and close to a wall of precariously balanced stones. Then she went off for a conference by the well with the other women who, as they washed mushrooms and pulled up the buckets, studied me with sidelong glances.

I was amused, but tried to convey humility and plain human need. Among these wholly civilized creatures I felt no fear, as I had among the men and their dogs. Part of what amused me was a different well, in a village in Uganda, where tall and graceful black women strode from their cottages dressed only in necklaces and bracelets, balancing jars as shapely as themselves on their heads. That well in Uganda had been a noisy, a raucous place in comparison to this, but the curious glances and the whispering were the same.

To my surprise and pique, I did not get fed, and no one paid any attention to me for the entire morning. I sat and waited, or strolled the little plaza, watched a handful of children chase a goat across a field, listened to the dogs bark and whine to be fed or set free. Finally I convinced myself that I was mad, that I should get back to the caravan at once and give up this place and my silly curiosity about it. What adventure or discovery was possible, after all, in a little mountain village where hardship, history, the weather and necessity compelled every person to spend the day foraging and scraping, scrounging and digging? I was unwelcome, and this was a working day.

I was about to make the trek up the muddy trail when the door on a nearby hut was pressed open by two small men in yellow robes and fur caps. One came directly to me, took me by the elbow and escorted me into the hovel where the other man still stood, patiently holding the door. They seemed serious in the extreme, as if in mourning, or as if I were being led into a judge's chamber to be tried for murder.

Here my life changed, in this little room. A huge dog roared up snarling from a corner, but was knocked aside by one of the men and commanded into a whimpering silence. A hole in the roof permitted a shaft of sunlight to fall on a small table and also allowed the yellow smoke from a dried dung fire to drift out into the cold blue air. A third man sat at a little table with his eyes closed and his teeth bared, as if he were enduring great pain. Why? I wondered. I expected him to make some gesture of welcome, but he only rocked and grimaced, and sometimes drew in his breath sharply.

By a gentle pressure on my shoulders, I was told to sit down across from the man, and though the dog growled low in his throat, I did so. On the table before me were a knife and a small jade dish, and what I took to be the white, fibrous stems of the large red mushrooms I had seen earlier in the old woman's apron.

In a moment, one of the robed men placed a wooden spoon and a cup of curdled, white, custardlike substance before me —goat's or yak's curds, possibly a yogurt, I thought—and by mimicking the motions of eating, communicated that I should consume it. I bowed as well as I could sitting down, picked up the spoon and brought the cup to my mouth.

Nothing in my experience prepared me for this. I had eaten preserved duck eggs, sea cucumbers in a black, tar-like sauce, eels, frogs, snails, squid, fermented turtle parts, grasshoppers, shad roe, lamb's eye, raw fish—possibly even dog, and almost certainly horse meat (in Thailand and Spain respectively). Food interested me as a fundamental expression of a community's creativity, its culture, and I had never been disgusted by its seeming strangeness. But this food outwitted and nauseated me. It smelled of vomit and, yes, urine, and my stomach refused. Involuntarily I held it away from me, and one of the men in the shadows of the hovel laughed. The dog growled and was hushed. I waited for my mind to clear and thought of cheeses I had tried with similar aromas, kidneys, fermented gruels.

The man across from me was in such agony that he fell on his side with a groan and this added to my disgust a fear that I might also be poisoned. What was his difficulty? Neither of the other men in the hut seemed the least perturbed by this development and, in fact, when I appealed to them, only indicated again that I should eat the substance before me.

This time I managed, I gobbled the vile gruel down and by an extreme effort of will managed to keep from gagging. For a second I felt a wave of heat and dizziness pass over me, but this was followed by an astonishing clarity of sight, like that which sometimes accompanies a fever, and I could only think, Well, this is the end, I've done it now. The dog eyed me coldly and the hairs of his pelt seemed like spikes, each one hard as wire, or needles, and I was careful to speak softly what gratitude I could mutter to my hosts. The presence of the dog was like a gun at my head. I began to resent it with a ferocity surprising, and even frightening, to me. I imagined tearing the dog in two, ripping him apart by his jaws, and was startled by the vividness of this fantasy: it seemed to leap from my head and play in the air like a movie, a hologram, or a dream made visible. The vision disappeared with a snap.

The robed men spoke to each other in low, gentle voices now, and their apparent calm quieted me. I thought it was odd I should be able to hear us all breathing. In a moment a door was opened to admit another man who acknowledged me with a bow I tried to return. As he bent forward, his yellow cap seemed to leave a streak of color in the air, and when he talked he waved his hands like a conductor in graceful patterns that I found stupidly but thoroughly engrossing. I couldn't get enough of watching his hands fly through the air, like butterflies. Had he been brought in just to amuse me with the cleverness of his hands? He sat near me at the table and the robed men spooned some of the gruel I had just taken into a cup and set it before him. He grimaced and laughed, then drank the stuff down quickly, and, as I had done, struggled to keep from choking.

Now I understood. I knew I was going away. The man on

the floor, in an act of ultimate generosity and hospitality, had eaten the mushrooms, the red ones flaked like candy, and then taken the poison into his body. It was his urine, perhaps also his vomit, we drank in the curds, which contained the drug which would take us away, but not the poisons which wracked him. When I realized this, I stood up in wonder and gratitude at last and crowed "Ah!" The sound of my voice echoed from the walls.

In the course of that afternoon and night, perhaps a dozen men came to the hovel and drank the potion, and fell, with me, into the lap of God. What shall I tell you? That I saw rainbows around the teeth of these men, and those of the dog? That some of these men melted before my eyes and became glistening pools of oil on the floor? That when I stumbled outside of the hut I realized at once how ruined the world was, how barren the hills, how infinitely sad the cry of the yak in his little pasture? And even so, the grass swirled away from the village in designs that would astound a lace-maker; every rift in the soil was a stitch in a fabulous, living carpet.

A butterfly landed near me, quiet, unafraid or unaware of my secret presence, and remained still for my inspection, and when it opened its wings the air filled with eyes, hundreds of eyes that floated off the wing of the butterfly and sparkled in the air until, to my sorrow, the little creature tumbled away in the wind. The yak bellowed again. The sound of his cry was like the peal of a tremendous bell, but I could see it now, too, a blue, shimmering cloud that welled up out of his lungs and shook the sky around him, and around us also, who were caught in the sudden web of his voice and his sorrow. The ruts in the road teemed with golden light, and when the night crept over us I could feel the planet turning and tilting, the stars came out in such a spray that I could only grovel before them. There was no reason for not falling out into the sky. It could happen at any moment. And as I lay in the talking grass and put my hands to my temples, I could see my brain in my hands like a great glowing pumpkin, a city, and my heart became visible, too, a red dragon that would walk away from me if it could, except for the net of vessels that trapped it, and this now transparent prison of the skin.

I think it was the moon that smothered me, and I sank down with a cry. This is where I died, near a hovel and a yak in Tibet.

When I regained sanity, or to put it better, my habitual consciousness, the sun was stoking the rim of the mountains with a scarlet fire. I floated and stumbled back to my own camp in what seemed a riot of wind and water, though of course it was only the grass that surrounded me, and not the seas parting, only the talking grass. I came into the compound where all were asleep, and shouted, and awakened everyone in a kind of mischievous glee that they were all still there and their bodies were still pumping blood and extracting oxygen from the air. They complained and joked, and cursed me. I spoke a while to a donkey who seemed wise and faintly bored, and to the *sherpa* who understood at once what had happened: "The red bull?" he asked.

"Yes!"

"He is mighty." The *sherpa* smiled.

The Chinese sponsors tried to make sense of my absence and my fussing. But I had nothing to say that would seem coherent to them, my thoughts blew about like milkweed seeds on a purposeless wind. The Chinese were angry and grew officious. By noon, our trek was cancelled and we were being herded, hurriedly, back to the city where we would be safe from the unregenerate farmers and their mushrooms. All the way back, I wore the woman I had been cruel to like a jewel around my neck. That she had eyes and could see the world, and still not see it, made me weep. "Look!" I kept saying. "Eyes! How marvelous! *Eyes!*"

I think some of those who drifted away from my company after this trip would tell you I went mad, I had a "nervous breakdown," was poisoned, endured a "psychotic episode," a break from reality, schizophrenia. All that nonsense. They think I am afraid of the night now when I am only reduced to astonished misery by the hanging ocean of the stars. Every diamond drop of rain reflects the world. Should I *not* shout when this occurs?

Now I find money humorous. Really, it is as plastic as paint, as I said. I have sold my museum pieces, my historical junk, have given it away. Now I chase the mushroom wherever the conditions are promising: in America, in the Northwest, where the Indians knew about it, though for centuries they have ignored it, as if their system is too tired now to have any effect from it other than to be driven mad; in the Himalayas; in northern India; maybe—I hear from a devotee—in Japan. It comes up through the brown, acid soil, high in the mountains, under the birches or pines, like a fist covered with fleece. Snowy child of the monster! The poison in it destroys the blood, and those of us who love each other and this pursuit take turns eating the pulp. How like God, to give a vision and then kill you for it!

And I am in pain, of course, not for finding God in a hovel, but for the botching of our everyday lives and our historical potential. My only solace is to think that, like the suffering man in the hut, we are meant to absorb the toxins of the times so the future may absorb a little measure more of bliss. If only we knew! Are we shamans, or silly drunks?

If only we knew!

One Up

The Fat Man had graceful hands and he held his cards in an almost effete way, or as if he thought them valuable, full of secrets, and he studied them as another might study cuneiform, runic characters, cabalistics, and somehow his eyes never lost the curious attention, never displayed certainty or doubt. Neither was the Fat Man one who displayed the coarser kinds of gambling dynamics, taunts, jibes, distractions, teasing. He played simply, as if no two hands were alike and each had to be rediscovered.

Of course he was a dangerous player. If usually conservative, he would also take risks. His presence in a game gave Roosevelt several feelings at once: that it would be a serious game, demanding constant attention and calculated betting; that if the Fat Man lent a certain ease to the table, was almost a comforting figure, then the Fat Man was also deception itself, for the truth of the matter was that he remained unknown. Some people called him Browny. Some people called him Fats. He had no past, and yet it was rumored that, with those delicate, manicured hands of his, he had killed. Perhaps there was another creature inside that composed and attentive facade, but Roosevelt saw no outward sign of it.

The Fat Man dressed like a gambler, like a street sharpie, with a snap-brimmed gray hat with a black and yellow striped band around its crown; he wore white shirts and thin black ties, and a gray and white checked sportscoat; his black leather

shoes always gleamed. Roosevelt had seen him shoot pool, too
—where he could hold his own, but which was a game also
that obviously did not hold the same fascination for him as
poker, which he was addicted to, Rosey thought, in the way of
an opium smoker who has plenty of opium and a sure line of
supply—like the man in Saigon they had called Moto-wan, or
Papa-san Wan.

The Fat Man laid down his cards now with a little flourish,
so that the edges snapped on the table. The tips of his fingers
remained on the borders of the cards, too, like a Ouija reader's
fingers on the moving pointer. "Three ducks," he said. Roosevelt folded his two pair, aces and fives, and tossed them a little
hard and recklessly into the discard pile. He had six dollars
left. He was on the edge of disaster. In this game, six dollars
could be easily overwhelmed. He tossed in his fifty-cent ante
and waited for the next round of cards to be dealt. Maybe lightning would strike. He picked up his cards and thumbed them
open, but lightning did not strike. When the Fat Man opened
the betting for two dollars, floating the bills into the center
of the table with a flick of the wrist, Roosevelt left his cards
on the table and pushed back his chair.

"You leavin', Rosey?" the Fat Man asked.

"Yeah."

"Better luck next time."

"Screw ya."

"You goin' to play some nine-ball?"

"Maybe."

"Don't go away sore," the Fat Man said. "Have a beer on the
house."

"Ain't thirsty." Rosey stood behind the chair and watched
the game progress. It was a cut-and-dry hand won by Smitty,
the chauffeur, whom Roosevelt did not particularly like, with

a simple pair of aces. Smitty, his black face gleaming, gloated over the take as if he had won a great deal of money. As far as Roosevelt was concerned, it was a pot wasted. Smitty would do one of two things if he won fifteen or twenty dollars: quit and go drinking or blow it on a bluff that everyone else knew was coming.

In a way, Roosevelt felt sorry for Smitty. He really didn't know what was happening. Everybody knew his game, and yet he still thought he was being slick. He was at the other end of the scale from the Fat Man, and yet somehow just lucky enough to keep coming back for punishment. Nobody discouraged him because he primed the pump, thanks to his job, and also, thanks to his job, had plenty of free time in which to make his contribution. Maybe, Roosevelt had thought, I should take the brother aside and set him straight. And yet he didn't like Smitty and thought he got what he deserved for being such a fool, and never acted on this impulse. Smitty was a grown-up and Rosey let him hang.

Yeah, sure, he thought now, and who is it going out the door broke today?

Rosey drifted down the main street of the neighborhood feeling irritated, as if he had needles under his fingernails. All morning long he had held second-best hands, cards good enough to bet on, but not, by chance, good enough to win. Three times the Fat Man had stung him for about twenty dollars, and the hands Rosey won did not come close to taking up the slack. "Don't gamble if you can't afford to lose," the Fat Man was fond of saying. He said this to everyone who found his way into his daily game. Once he told Rosey, as they sat alone at the table playing gin rummy and waiting for enough men to drift in to start a poker game, "About the only thing I know about you, Rosey, that I would tell you, is that you are not a sucker. I believe we can say with confidence that you are not a sucker." He had chuckled when he said this curious and yet obvious thing.

Or was he pulling my leg? Rosey wondered now. Maybe he sees me the same way I see Smitty. The thought made Rosey momentarily furious. He hated not to understand things, not to know how things worked. He hated to think the Fat Man might have his number.

There was a lot of broken glass in the gutter lately, Rosey observed. Why the hell can't they clean this goddamned street up? He hated things not being clean. When he showed up at Pointer's Rack and Cue now, the attendant took a brush out from beneath the counter, ambled down to Rosey's table and brushed up all the crumbled chalk dust and raised the nap on the deep-green felt. He did this even when Rosey joined a game in progress. That was good. Rosey appreciated it, and tipped him well. Pool was beautiful when it was perfect, and clean, the balls gleaming in the lights, the felt unmarred by scars or spots of grime, the rails without any ragged edges, fraying, bald patches. An immaculate table and good equipment left you with no excuses. The game was merciless enough, physics incarnate, determinism manifest. So why couldn't they clean up the streets? Why did the garbage men leave so much detritus behind? Didn't people *notice*?

Rosey came into the pool hall jangling, letting his anger bubble up. The attendant broke his attention on a men's magazine long enough to hand Rosey his cue from a rack, which he had to unlock first, on the wall behind him. Rosey turned the magazine around so he could observe the foldout the man had been studying.

"Look here," he said, tapping his finger in the center of the page, "these white women got that sweet thing, too?"

The attendant, who was white, wrinkled his nose and

handed Rosey his cue. "That's what it looks like," he said. "But you couldn't prove it by me."

"I ain't surprised." Rosey snatched his cue.

"I'll be down in a minute to brush that table for you."

"Right." Rosey's irritation crescendoed because, along with a couple of the regulars who showed up to play nine-ball on their lunch break, today there was the Sailor, hobbling around the table, his crutch against the wall. Good old Sailor leaned his head of black curls over the table and jabbed away, shooting the ball too hard to make good sense, but also rifling the shots in and finding good position.

Rosey could never make up his mind about the Sailor, whether he was just damned lucky or whether he was good, and faking clumsiness. The Sailor was, in the way he played pool, like the clerk on the command ship Rosey had been on, who typed with two fingers, but at a monumental pace. Everything the Sailor did was wrong. He didn't concentrate, he shot too hard, he leaned all over the table reaching for shots, tried ridiculous combinations—and yet he always seemed to make money. He made a lot of shots that counted, and he never felt pressure. He played as if he didn't give a damn if he lost everything he owned, and Rosey thought it was probably true, that he didn't care.

His whole crap-filled being spilled out on the table when he played, Rosey thought. A big part of his game was mouth. The Sailor wouldn't shut up and he couldn't stop either a constant dither of insults and challenges that he didn't seem to understand were, for a white boy of his particularly obnoxious stamp, genuinely provocative and dangerous. By some miracle, he had not yet been thrashed in Pointer's, though he had also come in on more than one occasion with bruises under his eyes or scabs on his lips. Maybe he thought being crippled would save him; or maybe—Rosey thought this the likeliest

—he wanted to be beaten, to be punished and humiliated. It wouldn't exactly be easy—the Sailor had biceps that swelled the sleeves of the gray T-shirts he perpetually wore, a broad chest and, Rosey was sure, a thick, bull-like forehead. He could take and give a few punches. Like some punchy fighter, he'd enjoy the process of his own murder if he could meanwhile just get in a few licks of his own.

And the Sailor lied. Rosey hated him most not just because he lied, but for what he lied about. Rosey had seen men maimed and killed in combat. He had seen too much of it. The Sailor had told him, as he told everyone, that he was crippled in Viet Nam. But Rosey had a habit of suspicion, and of curiosity, and he had found out the truth, that the Sailor's injuries had resulted from an automobile accident, caused by the Sailor's drunkenness, and which resulted, too, in the deaths of a fifty-seven-year-old mechanic and a sixteen-year-old girl. The mechanic was in the other car, the girl had been in the Sailor's.

Steebs was his real name. And Steebs, in Rosey's book, was a lying, motormouth motherfucker cruising for a concussion. He had done a little time for the accident, two years, and he was not allowed to ever drive again. Rosey figured that the Sailor hadn't paid enough for those deaths, and was hell-bent on self-destruction. He pretended to be bitter about his disabilities, about his bad luck and the treatment he got as a veteran, and he pretended to hate the world. But Rosey was one up on him, because Rosey knew what Steebs really hated, that he could never shake it, never with booze, never even with supreme concentration on the billiard balls, not even when someone he angered and provoked obliged him by stunning him into unconsciousness.

Steebs' disease, his cancer, was himself. The only real cures were total. Rosey understood his recklessness, his zeal for insult, and he felt used and nauseated by it. In spite of himself, he loved taking Steebs' money, loved beating him on the tables, and was infuriated when, rare occasion that it was, Steebs came out on top. Do Steebs and everybody a favor and murder the son of a bitch, Rosey thought now.

Rosey filched a piece of chalk from a neighboring table and carefully covered the tip of his cue with the sky-blue dust. The Sailor hobbled around the table, blasting away.

"You want to get in this shit?" he said to Rosey. "Five-ball pays a dollar, nine-ball pays two."

"Hear my knees knockin'?" Rosey said. "I'm so scared, I might lose a buck or two."

"It's for a good cause," Steebs cackled. With a gentle tap, he knocked the nine-ball into the side pocket. "Sorry about that," he said to the two men staining the wall with the heels of their shoes, a young kid named Landry who was supposed to be in school and somebody they called Lefty, a seaman who was only irregularly on the scene. Lefty was a little nuts. He kept opening his eyes as wide as possible, then squeezing them shut, and he wore a manic smile perpetually on his coal-black face.

Rosey wondered if the sea had made him crazy, or if you had to be a little crazy in the first place to want to go to sea. Rosey had found the big boats of the Navy boring as hell to travel on, and he wondered what Lefty's life was like as a freighter rat, grease monkey in overextended engine rooms. The difference between the Sailor, Steebs, and Lefty, the seaman, was vast: Steebs was a screwed-up veteran on a big guilt-trip; Lefty was an ocean addict, virtually a hermit, so concentrated in his own crazy self that nothing was very real to him—certainly not the pay he could be throwing away again—except the constant undulation of the sea.

"Your mama ain't callin' you?" Rosey said to Landry, the kid.

"Don't 'mama' me," the kid said.

"You ain't got no money to lose anyway," Rosey said. "Unless you been beatin' old ladies."

"Kiss my ass," Landry said.

"How much you owe this Sailor motherfucker?"

"I don't know."

"You'd better know."

"I don't know. Seven dollars."

The Sailor laughed. "Right now it's ten dollars, kid. I got 'em both last time, five and nine."

"Yeah," the kid said. "We'll see."

"You ain't got no credit here," Rosey said. "You got ten dollars?"

"Hey!" Landry said. "Who are you? FBI? Rockefeller? Mind yo' business."

"I'm going to win the next five games," Rosey said. "You got fifteen dollars more than the ten you already owe?—twenty-five dollars?"

"You know I'm good for it."

"Bullshit," the Sailor said. "If Rosey's getting in, let's settle up now."

"Why you pickin' on me special?" the kid wailed.

"Get serious," Rosey said. "You got the money or don't you? Pay up or I'll have Charlie toss your ass out of here."

The kid threw some bills on the table. "Six dollars," he said. "That's all I got."

"Not enough," the Sailor said.

"It's what I *got*."

Rosey stabbed his finger into the kid's chest. "I told you about that. I told you before. You can't play if you can't pay."

"He lets me," Landry said. "He said my credit's good, so get off my case."

"Not true," the Sailor said.

Rosey threw four more dollars on the table. "O.K., Sailor,

you're square. You owe me four," he said to the kid. "But you're through for today." He took the kid by the shoulder and pushed him toward the door. "Let me tell you something," he spat. "The Sailor's dyin' to mix it up with you, man. He'll tell you any shit to get in a row with you. That's his weirdness. Believe me. Don't let him work his weirdness on you."

"I'll kill that sucker," Landry said.

"It's a Bozo game." Rosey let go of the kid now. "You can't let him Bozo you. You have to be cool, you have to be clean, have no debts, ask no favors, ever. Once he gets you sore, he keeps pressing it until you pop. That's his game."

"I'll pay you back," Landry said.

"Do you hear what I'm telling you?"

"Yeah, Rosey, I hear you."

"I don't pay any more of your bills."

"Right."

Landry banged out of the pool hall, and the clerk came down to brush up the felt as Rosey returned to the table.

"Leave some nap on it," the Sailor said. "The table's fast enough."

"You know we don't allow gambling in here, don't you?" The clerk stopped brushing and looked deadpan at the Sailor.

"Don't worry about it," the Sailor said. "If we see any gambling we'll let you know."

"Keep your money off the table. I mean it. There's all kinds of assholes running around here today. I don't want to be shut down again. Do me the favor." He raised a cloud of blue dust as he finished his chore.

"Sure as shit," the Sailor said.

Rosey was breaking his own rule, with only two dollars left, going into a game with the Sailor and Lefty. He was doing exactly what he had told the kid not to do, but he felt so sure, as he racked the balls, so confident today, so angry that he could concentrate hard enough to see his own face reflected in the shine on the balls. He could see right through the balls today. There was no way he could lose. Today, he could talk to the balls, and they would pay attention and do his bidding. He imagined each of the games before they happened. Once he got a break he was going to stay on the table for a long time.

"Pretty enough," Rosey said as he smashed open the rack and saw just an orange blur of the five-ball vanishing into the corner pocket. "Pretty enough."

Rosey left Pointer's with thirty-five dollars and hustled the three blocks back to the Fat Man's game. He was tired, but he figured his luck was running good now, and he had a settled, savage feeling in his gut after stinging the Sailor so well, well enough to get him bitching and whimpering, Bozoing himself. He had cut Lefty pretty deep, too, but Lefty didn't know any better, and, like the chauffeur, you had to have Lefties in the game to spice it up a little bit, throw in a wild card, build up the pot. Lefties made the world go 'round. Fringe cats, between the money supply and the streets. Hooray for Lefties. Hooray for trickle-down.

The Fat Man was sucking his teeth and studying his cards when Rosey came in. There was a big pot in the center of the table, and a big pile of money in front of the chauffeur, too. The other two players leaned back in their chairs, sipping beer and waiting. One of them nodded to Rosey and said, "Smitty's gone crazy."

"Definitely," the other man said. "Dude's on a *roll*, Jim."

The Fat Man counted out several bills and dropped them into the pot. "I'll just call you, Smitty."

Smitty, laughing so hard the tears rolled out of the corner of his eyes, laid down his cards. "Three aces."

The Fat Man leaned across the table and spread Smitty's

cards with the tips of his fingers. "Right, three aces." He dropped his own cards face down on the table and sat back as Smitty raked in the pot. "Your deal, Wallace," he said.

The man he had spoken to raised his hands in mock surrender and said, "I'm out."

The other player pulled back his chair. "Same goes for me," he said. "Smitty raised hell with me on that last one."

"And I'm steppin' out myself," Smitty said. "Can't play three-handed."

"Don't split now," Rosey protested. "I just got here."

"Time to go," Smitty said. "Time to grab hat." He strangled bills and stuffed them carelessly into the pockets of his tan suede jacket.

"What you got to spend your money on?" Rosey asked.

"Redhead," Smitty laughed. "Lord, what a day! Them cards were so good to me today!"

The Fat Man glanced away when Rosey looked at him. His eyes just sort of disappeared, acknowledging nothing. Maybe there was a trace of disgust in the way he chewed his gum, but then he leaned back in his chair with his hands behind his head, stretching and yawning.

"Don't go away sore," the Fat Man said. "Have a beer on the house."

But nobody stayed. There was a momentary clatter of men on the stairs, and then a smoky silence. The Fat Man yawned again and started to shuffle the cards.

"Damn," Rosey said.

"He pulled one out of his ass, what can I say?" The Fat Man started to deal Rosey a hand. "Gin rummy. Nickel a point."

"No way. I can't play for stakes like that," Rosey said.

The Fat Man continued to deal. "It's O.K., Rosey. Your credit's good with me."

Rosey sat down and picked up the cards. He felt a little sick, a little betrayed, found himself hissing at the Fat Man, the un-expected words burning out of his mouth, "What the fuck is it you know about me? Huh? What the fuck is it you think you know?"

The Fat Man chewed his gum like a cud. He fanned his cards. He said nothing.

Buck and Tracey
Go Walking

1.

Tracey "The Tigress" Wynn and Buck Lord are walking down Henan Xi Da Jie, a street thronged with bicycles, taxis, minibuses. A kind of oboe is playing, but weirder, more insistent, like a snake charmer's melody. The music makes the new, the simply unfamiliar seem strange. The sky is a crisp blue above the curved peaks of the buildings which line the street.

Tracey is looking good and has intended to look good. She never goes out on the street without intending to turn heads, even with Buck along, or maybe especially because he is along: because she knows it excites him and makes him a little jealous, a little more in her sway, and it flatters him also to think he has what other men want. But the truth is he doesn't "have" Tracey. She is loaning herself to him for a while, as long as it is expedient and pays off. She has no intention of living forever with a damned spy. And meanwhile she can show off a little because Buck is there to ward off any unwarranted attentions, anything like real contact, or speech.

What Tracey has to show off is plenty. She is tall and blonde with a placid face that she turns into a mask of boredom. Her blue eyes recede behind little slits, and it is a trick of hers to grasp your attention by opening her eyes wider, to let you know she is observing you. Then there is this little aura of secrets being traded. You may blush if you are not careful.

Her lips are full and she pouts a little to emphasize them. She knows how a woman's mouth can make a man swoon with fantasy and she knows in fact, concretely, from considerable experience that her mouth and tongue can be agents of ecstasy. She has used this knowledge on only the very most special occasions. Buck has received only a portion of this expertise. The full expression of her wisdom would be wasted on him, because he cannot surrender. All the same, she hints at the knowledge sometimes in the way she pouts, or in a seemingly unconscious little flicker of tongue.

Tracey leaves a portion of her neck exposed, and a portion of her shoulders, because she cannot stand being closed in by anything and because she knows it invites at least a fantasy kiss. For the same reason, she almost never wears a bra, the exceptions being when she wants to calculate an effect. Her breasts are not large, but are firm and perfect for her size, and she considers them good friends and a source of pleasure. Buck is exceedingly fond of them. Tracey thinks it is stupid that women have to keep their breasts covered, unfair that men can bare their chests and women can't. In this strange country where she walks now with Buck at her side you cannot even show the bottoms of your feet, and curled toes are taken to be a symbol of orgasm.

Tracey's waist is slim, her belly taut enough to bounce quarters on. But she shows a little softness in the buttocks, just a little, so that if she runs in high heels you see her legs are athletic and lean, and her buttocks are aquiver. Altogether her overall leanness has nothing of the air of severe discipline or self-denial about it, and there are enough soft corners and sweet curves to telegraph her sensuality, some self-indulgence, a little hedonism. She would look terrible in leather and never wears it. She can be calculating and savor a revenge, but she is no sadist and has no stomach for torture. This does not mean she would not be capable of killing if the necessity were thrust upon her. Buck was relieved to realize this.

Tracey's intelligence is great, but of a peculiar kind. She is most sensitive to how people respond to her, and is therefore most comfortable in situations in which people must respond to her. She finds it hard not to be the center of attention, but also likes very much to be alone and can tolerate long periods of time with no intimacy to speak of, no socializing. She would, in fact, prefer being alone for a long period to being constantly in the presence of just one other person, and for this reason has preferred to live by herself even when most passionately involved. And although she has been perfectly intimate with both men and women, has loved, has given everything in a relationship, she still has hidden things away, and dreams of meeting a man someday with whom she can be totally uninhibited, totally real. A man or a woman, although she really would prefer it to be a man.

This means, of course, that there is a realm in which she demands privacy: to heal wounds, to establish or re-establish perspective, to be selfish. One thing absolutely Tracey is not: a martyr. And if men put her on a pedestal, she allows this only for ulterior motives and would never, never allow the pedestal to become her prison. She knows enough to know she wants a true life of her own.

Buck walks a little bit out of line, a little out of square. He does this in order to take in as much as possible: men leaning in doorways, faces in car windows, packages under arms, the lay of the land. He has dark brown eyes that never seem to engage you, are always looking past you, as if you might not matter much in the scheme of things, or as if you are and everything you say is being edited, everything unimportant to Buck—which is most of what you are and say—is being brushed aside. And yet he is not unkind, not unresponsive. He seems simply busy in the way his eyes are busy, looking everywhere at once, sorting things according to the secret purposes that rule him.

Even so, Buck is sometimes quite a talker. Not usually, but sometimes. It is as if a seam bursts, as if all the talking he has done has built up pressure and must find release. Then his eyes seem to be handling you, raiding you, rifling your pockets, invading your privacy. You wonder if these outbursts derive from moments of closure or simply from an overloaded sensitivity.

Buck loves Tracey to the extent that he knows it is possible for anyone who carries a gun and whose work is to ferret out secrets, who lives so insincerely and dangerously, can allow themselves to love someone else. He is glad that Tracey is so self-possessed, and it amuses him to think that she can enjoy him and his quirks and will be only mildly stung and irritated when it comes time for him to leave, or when he is arrested, or killed. So there are times when his own feelings of love disgust him, because he knows better, that they are futile and inappropriate. And in the meantime she is good cover and exquisite sexual relief.

Buck's face is square, hard-edged, except that his cheeks are soft. He has broad shoulders and slim hips, and fifteen years later would not look completely foolish in the Rutgers football uniform he once wore. Buck takes physical training seriously still only to the point he knows he might sometime have to endure a long passage, several days awake and moving on. If it comes to hand-to-hand combat, he would rely on several equalizers at his disposal, the pistol being the least and crudest of these. If he appears too fit, he throws suspicion on himself, or jealousy, and so, though he enjoys a modicum of rugged handsomeness, Buck does not draw attention to himself, and is rather used to fading out of people's awareness, like the cat you discover behind the curtains.

When Buck and Tracey make love, Buck is usually a little afraid at first to be so exposed, not to Tracey, but to anyone who might choose the moment to assail him. Therefore, though he is in love and eager and knows how thoroughly and well Tracey can satisfy him, he is sometimes slow to respond, which also works to his advantage since it seems to inspire Tracey. But once he is hard, he can allow Death to be the voyeur sitting on the headboard and take his time and pleasure, and be careful of Tracey's responses, and ask Death, "What would you like to see now?"

And Death says, "Turn her over. Take her from behind." And Buck does this, with gentle, firm pressure of his hands that the wise Tracey understands and allows. "Make her lick you and suck you," Death says, but Buck does not make Tracey do anything, only lets her know by fingers on the cheeks of her face, touching her lips, what Death is asking, and she, with throaty chuckle sometimes, complies, kisses down his chest or up his inner thigh and engorges him.

"Slap her," Death says.

"No," Buck replies. He knows Death wants always to spoil everything. More than anyone else, Death hates heroes, anyone, anything that gives life meaning. These he takes most virulently. Buck becomes more tender than ever, even though he is afraid and resents, resents thoroughly Death's presence and his requests to turn loving into politics, the sharing into a game of power relations.

"I'll get you for this," Death says.

"Oh go to hell." Buck cradles Tracey's buttocks in his arms, sucks her sex gently, licks.

"You're an animal," Death says. "Assert your power!"

As he licks now, Buck presses one finger, lubricated by Tracey's juices, slowly inside her, listens to the little moan of pleasure Tracey exudes, sustains.

Suddenly Tracey shudders, grips Buck's hair in her fingers, trembles, cries out.

"God!" she cries.

Death is gone.

2. More Tricks of Buck and Tracey

Tracey likes to crawl over Buck until his mouth is *right there* and she can lower or raise herself to adjust the pressure so that it is incredibly light or very firm, until Buck's lips are pressed back over his teeth. He holds her thighs in his hands and can be so very playful! *If only,* she has heard herself thinking, *he had another pair of hands and could do something with my lonely tits! Or another man, or woman, or both, to suck on them now.* Surely, in the beginning, she thinks, everyone fucked everyone else and all the time as often as possible. Surely in the igloos and the tipis and the caves there were five cocks and one woman and mouths and cocks and hands and cunts and mouths and cocks and fingers in everybody's everything and tits and cocks and cunts and tits everywhere.

When Buck frees himself he rolls over and enters Tracey from behind, using one hand to open her and massage *right there,* and the other hand finally covers a breast, the nipple gently held between fingers. *If only,* she finds herself thinking, *he had two cocks and one would be right there and the other just going up into just swelling into the notch and slowly in and one could feel the other in there, two in there, one from each direction, like two men could do it . . .*

Would that, she wonders, would *that* fulfill me?

3. Devotion to Cause

Buck is certain he hears the door handle click, and withdraws, presses Tracey down into the mattress, throws a blanket over her, and tells her to be quiet when she groans out a complaint. From the pocket of the shirt he had carefully draped over the chair back and placed close to hand, Buck takes the pen that is loaded with cyanide capsules and steps to the bedroom door, presses his ear against it.

"What is it, darling?" Tracey asks.

"Be perfectly quiet," Buck whispers.

What he hears is a little like what anyone hears when you put your ear to a conch shell—a hiss, a dial tone of random energy, a demon breathing in your ear.

Tracey rolls over and off the edge of the bed, lets herself down between the mattress and the wall, which is cold on her back. She puts her thumb knuckle in her mouth and bites down, hard, her cheek on the mattress, watches Buck in his absurd, alert crouch, his eyes still, uncapping a pen.

"No," Buck says. "I won't do it."

Tracey cannot understand who Buck is, or thinks he is, talking to. She bites harder on her knuckle, wishes only that he would return to the bed and allow her to stroke him, get him hard again.

Soon they are walking Henan Xi Da Jie, a handsome foreign couple, amazing the natives. They seem so sane, so permanent!

The Deaths of Strangers

Everything had been all right until Becker came down the thirty-eight stairs from his loft to find two men on the street in front of his door shouting at each other in Spanish and waving pistols. Wisely, he stepped back inside and watched the altercation somewhat sheltered, because the pistols started to pop only a moment later. The man that Becker could see through the mesh-protected window suddenly leaned far back and went down to his knees, as if praying or doing the Limbo Stick, put one hand over his eyes, and toppled.

Becker ran up three or four stairs, then turned around and ran back down, banged out the front door, and stood directly over the stricken man, his sneakers almost touching the tan khaki raincoat of the victim. There was an awful stain on the back of the coat. The man had curly black hair and a pencil-thin mustache, and he turned his head just slightly, just enough to look at Becker out of the corner of his eyes with supreme disgust and resignation. He coughed and the terrible stain spread, then broke out from under the coat in a thin red line that began to fill a crack in the sidewalk.

"Get away from there. You crazy?"

It took Becker a moment to realize the words were meant for him, and to find their source. Rudy Stein, his landlord, called again from the street-level electrical supply store that, along with Becker's loft and an adjacent florist, made up Stein's Twenty-fifth Street enterprises.

"Get in here, Becker. Those crazy bastards will gun you down."

Becker stumbled away from the bleeding man.

"Come on, Paul, *quick*. We called the cops already."

Becker complied slowly, taking a good look up the street where the other duelist had once been, but who of course had vanished by now—unless it had been the man in front of the Chili-dog House, the man wearing a camel's-hair coat and gesticulating frantically as he ranted into the receiver, or the man in the striped shirt piling into the taxi, or the man loping past the marquee of the Teatro San Juan . . .

"Becker-er!" Rudy shouted hysterically.

"Right," Becker said. He stumbled into the electrical store, half catching the reflection of himself in the door glass. "That guy isn't dead."

"They're sending an ambulance," Rudy said. "They asked me if an ambulance was needed and I said yes. You can't help him by staring."

"I know CPR," Becker said. "I took a course last year at the Y."

"Good for you." Rudy pulled Becker out of the entranceway so he could shut the door. "Heart attack is not his problem."

"If he stops breathing, I could help."

"Yeah, sure, Paul."

They waited, standing close enough together in the narrow doorway to hear each other breathing, and watched the downed man twitch occasionally, or try to raise his head. Two or three times people charged into the store asking to use the telephone, but Rudy told them, "We already called."

Now they could hear the sirens and Becker sighed with relief and confusion. He felt a little drunk.

"How much did you see?" Rudy asked him.

"I didn't see the other guy. I just walked into this gunfight and I kind of panicked for a second."

"I wouldn't get involved then," Rudy said. "It could mess up your life, you know, take up a lot of time. The other guy knows where you live, too, if he saw you come down the stairs."

"I'd testify if I saw anything," Becker said. "I would."

"I'll bet it's over some woman," Rudy said. "It always is with these guys. The sexual revolution hasn't hit Puerto Rico yet."

"You don't know," Becker said, "I don't know."

"Yeah, but it's a good bet," Rudy said. "I'll bet you it's over some woman. Either that or cocaine."

"I don't know," Becker said.

A black and white police car wailed to the curb. The strobing lights sparkled in all the electrical store glass—the doors, the windows, the lamps—and polished fixtures of brass and chrome. In a few minutes an ambulance also arrived, adding its red blips to the carnival of reflections, and Becker and Rudy stepped out to the street to watch the professionals carefully and efficiently settle the body on a litter and roll it into the van.

"I think he's gone," Rudy said. "I didn't see them put in an I.V. or anything."

"They didn't cover his face," Becker protested.

The police sat in the car at the curb a long time after the ambulance had left, scribbling on a pad and talking into the radio. Becker considered tapping on the window of the squad car and telling them what he had seen, but as he reconstructed the event, he realized he had nothing much to say that would be of interest. He tried pulling himself together a little and reinventing the reasons he was on his way out the door in the first place. A bus to Wells Street, to look around a couple of art supply stores. Raw umber. Red ochre. He was also thinking of a new pallet knife, a fat one. Then he had thought he might stop by Yesterday's Pub for a beer and a sandwich and to see if the Professor or anybody would be hanging out there. Sure. He could tell them about the shooting. About the scarlet oozing into the crack in the sidewalk. The milky glaze over that almond-colored eye.

Maybe the guy wasn't even Puerto Rican, Becker thought suddenly. Maybe he was Vietnamese. But no. Becker knew the difference. Besides, the men had been shouting in Spanish, right? Of course they had. Christ, get a grip on it, Becker told himself. Ten minutes haven't passed and you've lost it already. They had been shouting in Spanish. Becker wondered if that was a detail that would interest the police, but decided it was all too obvious a fact, unless you could understand what they were saying.

But I don't have a clue what they were shouting about, Becker thought. He didn't want to think about it. The guy had looked at him as if Becker were invading his privacy, not the least bit panicked—just sort of *ticked off*, Becker thought. The lack of anxiety in the man's face clawed at Becker's idea at how one should behave if ruined, and close to death. Becker knew very well how he would respond if a bullet slammed into his body: like a horse in a barn fire, hysterical as that.

On the bus to Wells Street the crowd seemed edgier than usual. Something was wrong. People weren't talking today, the usual music of Spanish and Polish and Yiddish had burned down to a kind of greasy silence. Two kids were smoking in the back, defying the driver or anyone else to confront them. Everyone seemed a little tired and distracted. Ordinarily, Becker could count on a little conversation on the ride downtown, but today when he took a seat next to an older black woman she leaned forward and put her head in her hands. Becker did not think she was crying. But she might have been. What the hell was wrong with everyone? he wondered. He found himself growing inexplicably angry, eager to get off the bus and walking.

On the street, Becker cruised along with more than usual

energy, a fierce, long stride that had the people approaching him sidling out of the way. Women Becker had known often told him he appeared angry, even at times he wasn't the least bit incensed, but simply thoughtful or a little worried or puzzled and trying to think things out. It had distressed him to think that women, especially, had found him intimidating, that women he had liked and had good feelings for would imagine him angry, dissatisfied and even dangerous when he was only lost in a problem, some puzzle of shapes or colors or images. People were quite ready to assume him violent, or possessed, because the mask of his face was somehow not properly connected to his heart. But today they were in line. He was angry, and he must have had it written all over him because people got out of his way, and he liked that just fine.

Becker did his buying quickly, in two different art stores. No wonder he never had enough reds. They were so damned expensive, he couldn't afford them in any quantity. He didn't want to worry about the cost of a color when he was making choices in a composition, and he didn't want to be always running out. Did he use so much red, after all? No wonder Picasso had a blue period. Blues were cheaper. Was this a supply and demand problem? What made red so precious?

Becker steamed into Yesterday's Pub, drank one beer quickly, then settled down a little when the next was served. He recognized a few of the people in the pub as regulars, mostly students and much younger than himself, but no one was there he knew well enough to talk to. Maybe the Professor would come in, maybe not. Maybe Richard would show up—which would be a laugh. Richard had taken Marge from Becker after Becker had taken Marge from Don, and before Gary had taken Marge from Richard. Becker laughed. That was not precisely the dynamic of the exchange, but close enough to reveal the all-essential pattern.

Becker had been Donald's friend when Marge had been Donald's lover. Then Donald had been arrested for possession of marijuana one night after a row with a traffic cop, and in the bar after strenuous, futile efforts to get Donald out of jail Becker and Marge had a talk. Becker had never listened to anything like it. Marge said she was tired of Donald, of all his hassles, that she had really wanted Becker to begin with. She wanted Becker now, and she wanted to be free of Donald. She wanted Becker to protect her from Donald's craziness, and she was in love with Becker. She had always been crazy about Becker blah blah blah. Oh, and Becker had fallen at once, and that very night sealed the pact. Marge moved into the loft and into his bed and left for work through the very mesh-covered door that Becker had seen the gunfight through earlier in the day.

Six months later, Marge ran off with Richard. Becker got the story later when, after eight months this time, Marge ran off with Gary. Richard told him he had never experienced such an aggressive, compelling come-on, that he was lonesome anyway, and easily swept away by her. To Becker it was all like looking down a hall of mirrors. He and Donald and Richard and even Gary had continued to be friends, he supposed, if you could call it that, if they were really that close to begin with. And Becker felt Marge had scarred him. He didn't understand her cycle, and he had felt strongly about her, and when he understood he was another convenient cog in her mechanical revolution, he was flattened. He hadn't really existed for her, hadn't been seen and understood and appreciated in the way he understood himself to be from the words she spoke and the vigorous sexual life they had led.

He wasn't yet truly comfortable around the women he met, and, he had to admit, generally expected disaster in a relationship. Fun, yes. But all temporary. He guarded himself. Your place or mine? He preferred their places, because he could always leave. They'd go to work and he would let himself out, no sighs or good-byes. *Whew!*

He hadn't thought about Marge for months and months. He wondered where she was now and who she was cleavering into submission. Some day it would have to stop, wouldn't it, that kind of cycle? Wouldn't somebody blow the whistle on her? Wouldn't somebody say, "I'm not interested in your games. Go home"?

The jukebox was irritatingly loud, but Becker ordered another beer and began to look around. A very pretty young woman was playing pool in the back with a punker, a skin-head in tight sailor's pants. The girl had shiny, brunette hair and a marvelous bosom, as Becker saw it, that served as a ground for a stupid, common beer advertisement on her T-shirt. The guy was exactly the type Becker would love to trap in a revolving door. He couldn't stand the idea of a swell-looking girl like the one playing pool now being the least bit interested in the punk. He was thinking he might just talk to her and see what he could stir up when the Professor walked in.

The Professor wore a big Garbo hat today, and wool knickers with outrageous purple knee socks. She carried a big canvas bag with a wide strap and all kinds of junk was spilling from the maw of the thing, including pages of computer printouts that flapped beside her like a flag. The Professor didn't seem to recognize Becker for a moment, or perhaps her elderly eyes were taking a moment to adjust to the dim light of the bar, and then she did a kind of double take that included the clogs on her feet, so that her surprise was accentuated by a little flamenco-like noise.

"Paul? Yes, Paul. How nice," she said, and immediately came to him and laid a hand on his arm.

"I was hoping I'd run into you."

Now the Professor smiled a polite, grateful smile. "Nice of you to say so anyway."

She had a wonderful way of engaging your eyes at once, Becker thought. They seemed held in place almost tenderly by the wrinkled skin that surrounded them, and her freckles ("age spots," she called them) spangled about them in a starburst pattern.

Becker helped her onto the bar stool. "Let me buy you a brandy," he said.

"I won't hear of it. Unless you're suddenly rich. I'm rich, you're not. That settles that."

"You're not rich."

"Comparatively."

"Yeah, well."

"Besides," she said, "believe it or not, I'm off brandy. Now it's Scotch. Awfully bourgeoisie, don't tell me. I tried it, I liked it. What can I say?"

"Are you having lunch?"

"I never eat. You know that."

"But you *must*," Becker said.

"At my age, it doesn't matter. I get all the protein I need from beer and pills."

"I doubt it."

"Well, don't worry. Do I look sick?"

"Not in the least."

"There. You see?"

"I may try it myself." Becker waved to the bartender, who simply nodded when he saw who was sitting next to him.

"Don't you dare," the Professor said. "You've got a good twenty years to go before you can misbehave like that. I've earned it."

"If you don't mind then, I'm going to have a burger."

"Of course I don't mind, except I wish you'd put something in you less fatty and gruesome than a burger."

"For instance?"

"Suit yourself. I'm not your mother. Besides, they don't have seafood here."

"I'm trapped. It's burgers or burgers."

"Oh, I love America," the Professor sang out. "We are the protein people. We jog. Can you imagine someone in Ethiopia jogging? And please don't tell me you're a 'runner,' Paul. I beg you."

"Not on your life," Becker said. "When I want exercise, I go to the laundromat."

"That's what I like to hear, dear." The Professor patted Becker's hand. "Really, I knew two men in their fifties who, in the interest of their cardiovascular systems, went jogging daily on the high school cinder track—where, of course, they both died, jogging, of heart failure. I recommend against it every chance I get. Of course my students won't listen. They never do. When it comes to health, I'm nothing but a Cassandra."

The bartender brought the drinks and waited patiently while the Professor rummaged in her bag for a little pink change purse which, when she snapped it open, contained a single twenty-dollar bill. The Professor hated change, Becker knew, and she always left coins on the bar, not simply as a tip, but because she found them a nuisance. And she never carried more than twenty dollars, "because if I do I just drink it up or spend it on drinks for pals, and because I can't stand the idea that some highwayman would get any more of my money than that if he dared to rob me."

Now they drank and talked small talk, the Professor complaining about her latest batch of students—not one of them like Paul had been, she assured him, "they are so damned serious about such narrow little ideas"—and the "numbing" committee work she had been stuck with the last few months. "I can't tell you how badly I long to retire," she said. "I simply do not understand these people—though of course they should have the right to choose it—who go on working until the day they die. In fact, I find them sad, so unimaginative. The idea of living on reduced income scares them to death, they say. Bah. What they're afraid of is not less money but more time. And more freedom. As an artist and self-actualizing person, Paul, I don't expect you to fully appreciate other people's fear of free time. But it is quite a real phenomenon, and if you were forced to spend half an hour in front of a television, ever, I think you'd begin to sense why."

"On the contrary," Becker said. "I understand the fear very well. I thought I invented it."

"Hardly!" The Professor laughed. "And forgive me, but I don't think you do understand. To go from a life of constant structure to one that is comparatively free-form requires some planning and invention, Paul, as so many discover when they reach retirement age—abiding leisure does not come naturally at all. Some suggest the elderly are afraid of dying, but I find myself willing to take my chances day by day. No, I say we are even more afraid of living because still, still, still, very few of us even know what this means. Do you follow me?"

"No," Becker said. "What I do understand sounds like the most crackbrained theory I ever heard."

"Hah!" the Professor snorted. "Crackbrained like Coyote, I suppose. I told you I was a Cassandra. How can I explain it to you? Well, suppose you lost both hands, God forbid. No more painting. You wake up in the morning and there you are."

"What a relief!" Becker said. "Then I'd be normal at last."

"Oh, you are so *perverse*," the Professor said, socking him in the arm. "I don't know why I put up with you."

"I don't know why either," Becker said. "I'm not even a good listener."

"You do seem distracted."

"I have been dying to tell you something. Something awful."

"And here I've been blabbering on. That wasn't fair. You know I love awful stories." Still, the Professor seemed to draw away from him a little, as if to prepare for a shock.

"I saw a man shot today, right in front of me, right in front of my door."

"Good heavens."

"He seemed only irritated about it, but mostly resigned."

"Someone just shot him right there?"

"He was in a gunfight," Becker said. "He had a gun."

"Lord in heaven. Do you know who shot him? Do you know what it was about?"

"They were arguing in Spanish, that's all I know," Becker said. "I didn't understand a word."

"Politics," the Professor said. "I'll bet it was politics."

"I'll be reading the papers," Becker said. "I'd really like to know myself what it was all about."

"Nobody is as passionate about politics as Latin Americans," the Professor said. "They believe politics has something to do with Truth, capital T."

"He was shot right in the chest," Becker said. "I think the bullet must have gone right through him."

"Politics is like faith with them."

"The blood ran out from under his coat and filled a crack in the sidewalk, then ran along that and into the gutter."

"I can see it had quite an impact on you," the Professor said.

"That was his blood," Becker said. "There is nothing redder. A little red stripe on the sidewalk. Still alive."

"Do you want to see someone about it? I can get some counseling for you."

"No, I don't want to see anyone about it," he said, trying to hold back his anger. "I want to know how he could just look at me like that with a bullet in him."

"Like how?"

"I don't know. *Contempt*, maybe."

"It wasn't meant for you."

"Contempt. Like he might have spit on anyone who might have tried to help. As if to say, 'I spit on your care.' "

The Professor put her hand on his arm again. "I don't think it means all this, Paul. I think you're projecting a lot of your own feelings onto that man. He was in shock, maybe also caught up in a little revenge drama, maybe also just too damned proud to show his fear."

"But you'd think that would be one sincere moment, wouldn't you? Just the minute before he died. He would stop playing?"

"He didn't believe he was going to die. Maybe he thought that, too, 'What a damned nuisance, to be shot like this.' Maybe death took him by complete surprise."

"I hope I find out what it was all about," Becker said. "The thing has really got me bugged."

"I can see that," the Professor said. "I can recommend a counselor."

"I'm not going to see any counselor," Becker said, quietly now. "I'm just going to go home."

"Call me if you like," the Professor said. "I'll be home with a batch of papers. Call me if there's anything I can do."

When he climbed off the bus at the Teatro San Juan, Becker knew he was going to have trouble. He tried to tough it out, but when he came within fifty feet of the doorway to his loft he was spun around and found himself heading the other way on the street. He pretended for a while that it wasn't happening, that he had just decided—not an unusual thing—to go into the Chili-dog House for a cup of coffee. He fooled himself enough that he even ordered a cup of coffee to go, and then made another assault on the doorway, with the same result. It was as if a great force field had been set up over the forty or so square feet where the man had lain, bleeding, and this powerful, invisible force blew Becker away from his home like a mighty wind. He tried to reason with himself, but it didn't work, and when he tried a third time to approach his door, and was repelled, he knew the Professor was probably right, that he was going to need help on this thing. He never needed help before. So why now? The idea refreshed his anger.

He could try the back way, but that meant climbing up on the trash cans full of discarded flowers, pulling down the fire escape, and then crawling across a narrow, shingled ledge to a window that was probably locked anyway. Come on, Becker said, that's crazy. The door's right there. I can't go through life crawling across roofs just to get home. I live there. This thing is not going to get me.

He made himself run toward the door, he was going to slip right through the terror zone and break its spell and charge up the stairs like a fullback busting through the defensive line. But it didn't work at all, he was slapped up out of his crouch and against the wall of the florist shop so hard that his body tingled and his hair crawled.

Why now? Becker wondered. *I didn't even know the guy.*

He wandered across the street, amazed at the volume of sweat pouring off him, breathing too hard and peering into one shop after another, into a bank of pirogies, a window full of tan loaves of bread, a department store, a travel agency emblazoned with Spanish signs in huge red letters, and finally into the Casa De Podre, where he stopped. The window display was made up of cards, Tarot cards, a crystal ball full of gray smoke, books on astrology and magic, small bones in a jar, and several dolls about the size of Becker's hand with scarlet sashes over their shoulders.

He stumbled in and a bell tinkled behind him. He wanted to smash everything in the place, every doll and relic and jar full of beads, rip every deck of cards to confetti. All this superstitious bunkum, rip-off hocus-pocus. But his anger diminished when a tiny, broad-shouldered woman with a red kerchief pushed through the curtains in the rear and confronted him. Becker laughed, feeling also a little sick, because it had been the diminutive size of the woman which cooled him down. She was like a big doll herself. He could have put her on his knee like a child.

"*Que quieres?*" she said.

Becker could not yet talk.

The woman waited patiently, folded her arms, eyed Becker with wet, black, beautiful animal eyes. Then she smiled and nodded. "Don't worry, kid," she said softly. "I got what you need."

A Sweepstakes Story

Today I received another sweepstakes entry letter in the mail which promised that if I read it through, every word, I would learn the secret of just possibly, it just might be *you*, Mr. Abel of Lake Pleasant, of winning fabulous sums. This gave me an idea.

Writers want nothing more than to have their stories read from start to finish. A six-page story that is thrown down in disgust by the reader at page three is a tragedy for the writer; the 500-page novel hurled into the fireplace at page two is an awesome calamity; if a reader falls asleep after the first six words, the writer of those words (unless he or she is a hypnotist) would surely contemplate suicide, or, even worse, changing professions. After I read the sweepstakes entry letter and learned that my key to possibly earning millions (or a compensatory yellow Cadillac, or a mountain escape hideaway, or a Marco Polo adventure vacation or one of a few zillion microwave ovens) was to "affix"—all official sweepstakes letters use this word—affix the gold seal to the red star on sweepstakes entry ticket number two, I decided to write a sweepstakes story.

A sweepstakes story is this: it offers a chance to win a prize to each and every reader who finishes it! THIS IS NOT A JOKE, MR./MS. READER! THIS IS AN ACTUAL CONTEST! If you finish reading this story, you will have an actual chance to win an actual prize. And if you want to know what that prize is, and how to win it, you only need to read on.

First, let me note that most sweepstakes entries ask you to purchase something. My sweepstakes makes no such suggestion. Of course, if you want to send money to the author as a tax deductible contribution to the arts, no objection will be raised and your sweepstakes entry will not be prejudiced in any way.

Most sweepstakes entries also promise fabulous benefits from buying their products. The letter I read this morning, for example, promised that if I subscribed to the publication sponsoring the sweepstakes I would receive information on how to save money on phone bills, college tuition and home insulation; prepare better, low-calorie, low-cholesterol, flavorful meals using real food; lose weight and become a sex object in my neighborhood; decide whether a career in forestry or computers is best for me; improve my marital sex life—the word **marital** was printed in boldfaced type, as if to emphasize that unmarried people should not read the article or even think about being married until they are already married; earn promotion and respect in my present job; laugh my way to better health; have a greener lawn and fatter tomatoes in only minutes a day and without using expensive chemicals; raise my children in a drug-free environment on updated Confucian principles; and . . . *much more.*

The letter also claimed that by reading the publication advertised I would understand why we need to be less hard on polluters and shoot Democrats on sight; why General Noriega is really an American patriot in the broadest sense; why pets, especially dogs, deserve to have as many constitutional rights as people; why it is the right of every American citizen to own bazookas and antiaircraft weapons; why automated telephone merchandising is a cure for the loneliness of the elderly; why Dan Quayle can't break 100 on the golf course and how America's heart goes out to him for that; how Millie had her puppies and other White House insider reports; how the Pentagon is just scraping by on a measly trillion-dollar budget—the promised article is titled "Military Belt-Tightening: Ow! Ow! and More Ow!"; and why we should let the prisoners worry about overcrowding in jails since they are the ones who got themselves arrested in the first place; . . . *and much more!*

As this piece of mine is only a simple tale, however, my sweepstakes cannot honestly make all these claims. The story can only do its best to make us healthier, wiser, safer, smarter, richer, sexier, richer, happier, younger, more productive, more pious, and more powerful. I know that some of you will object —but please, don't throw the story down!—that some stories make us feel sad, are written by Democrats or atheists, have existential overtones, contemplate death, dishonor, destruction, corruption, temptation, evil forces, junk food, antisocial behavior and unsocial desires. You are right, and I know this to be true also, and I have even heard it said that good writers make an effort to get at the whole truth of our lives and even resent comforting lies and sweet-smelling promises and exploitative half-truths.

But I ask you: could any sweepstakes story, even one like this one which offers a chance for a fabulous prize at the end, persuade its readers to continue on if it frankly and boldly declared itself to be the tool of the Devil or openly celebrated the Dark Side of life? How many readers would be willing to contemplate such a Frankenstein, even with a chance for a prize lurking somewhere in the pages ahead?

Gentle reader, ‹addressee› of ‹address›, let me assure you my story will not mention Chernobyl or Bhopal, South Africa or Richard Nixon, drugs or AIDS. It will be an MTV of a story. It will not assault your hopes and dreams and make you (or me, the hopelessly hoping writer) search for new hopes and new life and better, tougher dreams. No! That requires too much work, too much independence of mind and spirit, questioning our beliefs and habits, *sturm und drang*, self-confrontation, sleepless nights, a few tearful days, arguments, all the dues you pay to earn another *eureka* of the heart. This sweepstakes story will be a package deal, will reassure you, will tell you what to think, how to think, when and where to think. This story will not only offer a chance for a prize, it will offer *quick relief!* It will offer you a chance of something to hope for. A prize!

MR./MS. READER ADDRESSEE OF ADDRESS, ZIP CODE, THIS IS NO JOKE! This sweepstakes story offers hope.

Those of you still reading at this point: congratulations! You are on your way to learning the secret of winning a chance for the prize offered in this fabulous sweepstakes story. Let me make one further guarantee: this sweepstakes story will begin at the beginning, go on to the middle, and end at the end. It will begin with the perfect modern couple, married for 5.5 years, with 2.2 kids, living in a dwelling of 5.3 rooms, holding 1.6 jobs and earning 28.65 thousand dollars a year. They use tartar-control toothpaste, own a VCR and a dishwasher, one new and one used car, see 3.1 movies a month. The husband has eight ties and five pairs of shoes, two for jogging. The woman has eight bras and twelve pairs of shoes, including a pink pair of jogging shoes not used for jogging but to make it appear as if she might sometimes jog in pink jogging shoes. The children collectively own twenty-nine pairs of shoes, all of which are sneakers, except for two pairs for Sunday school, and all of which can be found at almost any moment somewhere in the 5.3 rooms of the dwelling place, usually on the stairs.

In the middle of this story, the perfect consumer couple reaches the end of the average life expectancy of the average American marriage and further contributes to the economy by turning their affairs, goods, chattel, and the fates of their children over to lawyers, judges, insurance agents, realtors and bankers. Just at this moment of trial and turmoil, one of the spouses wins fabulous sums in a publishers' sweepstakes! Yes! The sweepstakes is called "Beat the Pentagon!" and the amount of the award is equal to the entire budget of the Pentagon, plus $150,000 for early return of the sweepstakes entry card, and another $150,000 all-expenses-paid trip to New York where the family is filmed accepting the prize money from a television star with smudged eyeglasses and the personality of a day-old donut. This fabulous fortune temporarily reunites the family.

But further trials lie ahead. One look at the tax bill and the husband wants to secede from the U.S. and become a separate atomic power and economic force to rival Japan. The wife wants to make movies, help Third World nations become decent suburbs, and turn her children into rock stars. The children only want their parents to agree and once in a while take a trip to Disneyland. But the tension mounts even as trucks dump tons of cash and letters seeking donations or promoting vast economic enterprises on the front lawn and as the sixteen telephones jingle and jangle with calls from dreamers, schemers, thugs, politicians and smooth-talking businesspersons. Everyone in the family realizes, *My God! All this money causes as many problems as it solves!*

In the end of this story—well! The end of the story, dear reader, dear addressee of address zip code, that *is* the prize for reading this far! And you can have a chance to win it, free of any obligation whatsoever. All you have to do is send a postcard with your name and address to me, Box 223, Lake

Pleasant, MA 01347, and you will have a chance to learn what happened to Mr. and Mrs. Occupant and their 2.2 occupants who actually won "Beat the Pentagon!" sweepstakes and lived (choose one): . . . happily? . . . unhappily? . . . passionately? . . . curiously? . . . clumsily? . . . brilliantly? . . . ambiguously? . . . tumultuously? . . . elegantly? . . . philanthropically? . . . desperately? . . . wildly? . . . piously? . . . furtively? . . . other? (please explain) _____,
  ever after!

  Act now! The sooner you respond, the happier the ending will be!

Ghost Traps

Harper had seen Earl Ganneker twice now snaking away in his beat-up *Dog Days* from the pots Harper had set around the Gorilla Hole and along the channel off Potter's Landing. This didn't prove anything, but Ganneker was selling a lot of lobsters for a guy just breaking into the business and with so few pots in the bay, and Harper's own harvest had been notably declining since Ganneker came on the scene. You couldn't prove anything by that, but Ganneker was just the kind of guy who would be quick to point out the circumstantial nature of the evidence as he continued to pick you clean. Harper and "Earl the Pearl" Ganneker had gone way back, and, in Harper's way of expressing it, they had never enjoyed congenial relations.

Ganneker, Harper thought, couldn't seem to make up his mind what he was fishing for—lobsters, bass, flounder, cod—and that was part of his problem. Harper figured it was damn hard enough to learn to do any of them right, especially when conditions changed with every storm and every season, and here was Ganneker, all over the lot. He thought because he could handle a boat he could do any damn thing. Oh yeah, Harper thought. Let's see him try dredging scallops if he's so smart. He'd be tangled up like a bear in the wireworks. That's when you need a second hand, scalloping. Of course you really have to work and to know something then. You couldn't just go out and rip off somebody else's scallops and pretend you were a scalloper. You had to earn those the hard way.

On the other hand, Ganneker had had his problems. He learned bassing from his father, but then the bass stocks dropped off radically and they regulated the catch and the season so you couldn't make a living at it, really. The bass became a sporting fish mainly. Ganneker had tried guiding for them, but his heart was never in dealing with the public and giving away family secrets. He had taken one sport out and put him onto some great fish and the next thing he knew the son of a bitch had written it all up in a magazine and didn't even mention Earl's name. Harper couldn't blame Ganneker for switching out of a dead-end business.

But why did he have to take up lobstering? Too damn many lobstermen already and they all had the same problem: when they caught lobsters in plenty, the price went down and you weren't much better off than when the take was thin. And here comes Ganneker, adding to the supply, never mind where the lobsters were really coming from. Harper also couldn't blame the guy for wanting to stay on the water, like any true Ganneker, and the idea of Earl the Pearl in a factory was a joke, the man was so wild and rough-hewn. When he came back from Korea, he said he was never again going to take another order in his life, and he meant it. He wouldn't last a day in the factory, being told what to do and when to do it. Ganneker had no stomach for that.

Still. Pulling another man's pots. Some guys considered that a shooting offense. They'd motor up and unload a couple of shotgun blasts right into your hull. Let you think about it while your whole shop went down, and all the lobsters along with you. Harper never kept a gun on the boat, but he was thinking about getting his goose gun out of the barn and putting a tail on Mr. Earl the Pearl some morning. Just to keep him honest, if nothing else.

All the same, Harper told himself, without solid proof you

don't want to get tangled up with a ruffian like that. Harper admitted he might have been prejudiced about Ganneker by the rumors that clouded around like flies every time his name was mentioned in Warrens Bay. He had been pretty shot-up in the Korean thing and supposedly had come back addicted to painkillers and with a pretty generous disability settlement. If he had money, though, Ganneker didn't show it. He lived in a little room over Tiggard's Bait and Tackle and ate the specials at Tina's Diner next door. He didn't even have a car or a pickup, which you would expect a bassman to have, for getting down the beach when the weather was off for boating. His only possessions were *Dog Days* and his fishing gear, and most of that was given to him by his father. But of course you never could know what it cost to keep himself in booze and pills. Harper calculated that might have been plenty.

Folks said when Ganneker got to hurting—plates in his arm, plates in his head—he'd take those painkillers and hit the bottle, too, and he wasn't a man to be around then. Even more terrible in the eyes of Warrens Bay was that he'd pick out the worst possible company to do his drinking and pill-popping with, the welder Ray Stark.

Now Stark, Harper judged, would not steal a nickel from a millionaire. In fact, Stark didn't seem to notice money at all. If he had it, he spent it; if he didn't, he worked. He always seemed to have plenty of welding jobs or salvage jobs or something. As long as he was sober, Ray Stark was no worse than anyone else around, Harper thought. A big, round, muscular guy with the blackest eyebrows and beard, full of hogwash political opinions, he was pretty much like anybody else until he got a snoot full, and then he might go completely crazy. He wouldn't even know what he had done afterwards, but he had hurt people, and when the local cops got wind he was drinking they tried right away to lock him up before he did damage. They'd bust him for anything—dim taillight, pissing in a public way, socks being unmatched, whatever. Stark had been arrested by the Warrens Bay constabulary so often it had almost come to be a friendly proceeding.

Some people said Stark was sure to have some Indian blood and the alcohol poisoned him and set him off. Other people thought he was just dangerous anyway and drink only made him worse. And when Ganneker went drinking, he came and dragged Stark along, who normally couldn't be talked into it, and between the two of them they were trouble squared.

Some folks speculated that what these men needed was to find some women and settle down. To that notion Harper replied that as yet, thank God, there were not any women in Warrens Bay as crazy as that. Besides, Ray Stark anyway had once been married, back in the days when he had had his wits about him. He was even a pretty clever fellow then—built his wife a nice big house on family land out on Oyster Point (owned now by a New York psychiatrist) with a wonderful stone fireplace and hearth, all hand-laid. That house was built to last, and in fact had survived some storms that tore up the few other houses out there. Harper didn't like to think he was the only one around any more who remembered these things, and it made him feel old.

He reminded folks that it was right after Ray's wife walked out on him that Stark developed oddities and started prowling the bars. About that time, Earl Ganneker was not even around. He was on some Pork Chop Hill taking rocket fire up the ass. That's another thing, Harper reminded himself: he did serve his country, and he did pay a price. He didn't go looking to get all shot to hell, surely. He was drafted and Stark wasn't. That part of it was just a damned lottery.

I served, too, Harper thought. I tooted around Europe for four years on a tin can. Big deal. The only rockets he saw were in crates.

Rocket fire or no, you didn't go around stealing a guy's lobsters. If Ganneker wanted some of Harper's catch, or if he wanted to borrow a few traps, all he had to do was ask. You pulled a guy's pots and you were stealing his labor and his expertise, not just the lobsters themselves. That was the thinking around Warrens Bay anyway and if the rest of the world thought otherwise then that was another reason Harper liked living where he was, mean winters and all, Gannekers and Starks, and not much money to go around. Warrens Bay was not going to be on the news some night for inventing new and perverse ways to add to human misery. You could sit on your porch in the evening without hearing sirens and gunshots. If it was too quiet for some folks, well they could go back to New York or Boston and take their boutique and condo plans with them. The seeming stodginess of Warrens Bay folks just kept the traffic in crazies down, Harper thought. Got enough of our own in Ganneker and Stark. Don't need any imports.

He had to be fair on that point, too, Harper admitted. Ganneker and Stark were natives, out of old family lines here. Stark's ancestors went back to the days when Warrens Bay was Shotonomuck, an Indian name, and it was touch and go whether the town would be named Warrens Bay or Starks Bay for a while. The Warrens made it big in whaling, though, then the China trade, and the Starks may have had the numbers once, but they didn't have the knack for business. In fact, they kind of had a knack for the opposite. It was the Starks who thought they could reclaim Warrens Bay by digging a new channel on the other side of Oyster Point and connecting right into Glass Pond. And they did this on speculation, and of course the town fathers of that time let them give it a go.

Nine years later all they had was a big pile of mud and they never got a cent out of it.

The Warrens just moved out, ended up on Martha's Vineyard competing with the Coffins up there for whale kills and tons of cod. The Starks stayed right in Warrens Bay as it silted and shoaled up even worse than ever, and they went into the woods and hunted deer and became mechanics and preachers and grocers and gave up on the sea altogether. This was true even of Ray Stark now, who let everyone in Tina's know he never ate fish and just the sight of boats, even when he was out salvaging, made him seasick. He said nothing gave him so much satisfaction as cutting up an old wrecked boat. He felt it was one less misery in the world. Put that iron to good use, he said. Make bridges out of it, or tanks, something good like that.

The Gannekers were another story altogether. Some folks even believed—and it seemed plausible enough if you knew the family—that most of the Gannekers were conceived on boats, or born on boats, or both. Some had even died on boats, like Earl Ganneker's father, Martin. He had died right there in *Dog Days*, in a pile of bluefish and mackerel. They said when they buried him he still smelled like fish. Some said the grave itself smelled like fish to this very day.

The Gannekers even seemed out of place and awkward on the land. They couldn't walk straight or sit straight and were an outright danger to themselves running. Ray Stark had a moment of fame in high school as the fullback who gave people headaches when they hit him. But the Gannekers were not athletes, for the land fuddled them. In boats, however, they became quite graceful, as if connected to a part of themselves otherwise missing. Earl Ganneker was no different and if he couldn't dribble a basketball the length of the court, he had fished in weather, and brought in bass or halibut or some other treasured fish, when everyone else was holed up at Sandy's or Tina's listening to the reports and complaining and passing the time by writing checks to everybody they owed. If he had followed nature and gone with the Navy, Harper mused, Ganneker would never have been caught by rockets on a frozen hill. No, he should have stayed within the family genius, but the Army, in its wisdom, drafted him before he had made a choice. Now he really did have a wobble in his walk, even sober.

Years ago, when he was still trying to earn enough to buy his own boat, Harper had gone night fishing for bass with Earl Ganneker's father. Think of that, Harper reminded himself, because after all he had got the chance because Earl was in Korea. Time-wise that made sense. Earl was in Korea; Ray Stark was building a house for his lady love; Harper himself was farting around Warrens Bay being young and foolish. Martin Ganneker took him aboard because his own son was soldiering. Maybe, Harper thought, that's worth a few lobsters.

Old Martin left when the sun was dropping in the hills behind them and the water, which was mildly rocking them, looked to Harper just plain bloody. Martin knew his way around in the dark and he was careful about checking his meters and charts and he had a good working radio so that Harper quickly lost his fear of fotching-up on the famous Warrens Bay boulders. In fact, for Martin Ganneker, the boulders and ledges and shoals were just the right places to fish, and they drifted live eels down as deep as they could get them, where the tide ripped through ditches or boiled around the rocks or riprap and other structure down there, like the *Queens Full*, a Victorian tourist launch that rammed a hunk of granite and became a favorite fishing site.

Not that you could see a thing, Harper remembered. You just had to feel it all in the way the water flowed. And then, somehow, you kind of got a picture of things in your mind. You got so you could tie knots in the dark and you knew where your bait was. Sometimes the worst thing you could do would be to turn on a light, not just because it might scare the fish, but because it would ruin your night vision for a spell.

They were at the *Queens Full* when the fog started rolling in and Martin shushed Harper and then said, "Good," and rigged up a rod with just a bare treble hook and a sinker and started jigging like a madman. One after another he cranked in these chubby pogies, menhaden, which clattered in the bucket beside him. Then Martin showed Harper how to hook the pogies through the snout and live-line them, free-spooling them, right down the current into the rips you could almost not see flickering ahead in the blackness. When the bass hit, all Harper felt was a little tap, but the line burned out under his thumb until he clicked the reel handle over and the line tightened up and he socked them and the drag squealed with the momentum of their big-shouldered thrust.

Martin had been awake enough to hear those pogies splashing in the dark, and it paid off really well. To the four bass they had pulled out of the Gorilla Hole, they added three more apiece, all about forty pounds, all in the fog, not showing a single light, and in the most treacherous channel in Warrens Bay. Harper was gratified by how much attention Ganneker's father had paid to the drift of the boat even while working a fish, how he would correct the path of the boat with a little burst of the engine and would even tow the fish into deeper water to play it, and then circle around and make another pass. After all, they weren't out for sport. This was how Martin survived. He'd tow a fish now and then and no question.

On the way in, Martin was making what Harper thought was way too much speed for the conditions—total blindness —and no landmarks to be seen. The fog slicked everything and cooled his face and Harper kept trying to see anything at all, any glimmer or looming shape. Martin showed him where they were on the charts according to speed and time and readings from the depth gauge and they calculated carefully together. Martin figured the trip back would take an hour in the fog. But after forty minutes, he suddenly cut the engine, cut it off completely, and leaned over the transom, listening.

"I knew it," he said.

Harper heard it too then. About fifty yards ahead, water was thudding into something. Thudding and crashing.

"What the hell is that?" Harper asked. "Some scow?"

"Clemson Light," Martin said. "That's the breakwater. We're way south. The tide is running like a bitch tonight."

"Clemson Light?" Harper said in disbelief. "We'd better wait, hey?"

"We'd better wait," Martin agreed. "They got a lot of boats moored on this side of the breakwall and my insurance isn't paid." He laughed.

"How'd you know we came so far south?" Harper asked.

"I just felt that tide pushing us," Martin said. "You can't see that moon, but you know it's full, don't you?"

"Sure."

"What's that tell you?"

"Big tides."

"All right. Let's anchor and wash down these fish."

In the early morning, the sun stirred up a little wind, but it only blew the fog around. With its four hundred pounds of bass, worth its weight in gold even then, the boat responded sluggishly.

"We've gotta get these fish in there," Martin said. "They get too warm, nobody will buy them." He crawled toward the breakwall, still rattling with the waves tumbling into it. "We'll just try Clemson's," Martin shouted. "If we don't like their prices, we'll buy some ice and wait it out."

Harper sat on the gunwale, forward, staring into the fog, scared to death. They slipped by sailboats only a shade whiter or grayer than the fog around them, by draggers with huge fluorescent orange floats like party balloons glowing, by gillnetters with great coils of plastic netting looking ice-blue in the fog, and finally found the big red can 24 swaying seductively in the channel to Clemson's. Harper relaxed a little. If they smashed into something now, he knew he could swim for it, the breakwall only thirty yards off and on this side quiet.

Nobody was on duty on the dock because no one had imagined anyone would be moving in the fog that morning. Harper and Martin Ganneker had the pier to themselves, and when they walked out of the fog into the fish house the crew there, playing cards, jumped up in alarm.

"How about a box and some ice here?" Ganneker asked.

"You gotta be kidding, Martin," one of the men said.

"Come on. My bass are getting warm. Where's Tony? Does he want to buy any bass or do I have to take them back to the bay?"

"Where do you think Tony is, foggy mornin' like this?" another man said, settling down again and slapping a card on the herring barrel they had improvised for a table.

"Down at Sandy's with the rest of them."

"I don't think he even made it that far," the first man said. "He hasn't been married all that long, you remember."

"What have we got to do?" Martin said. "Get it ourselves?"

"Sure, why not?" one of the men said. "Ice is free this morning, shovel it yourself."

So Harper went into the rocking boat and gripped the big bass by their gill covers and hoisted them up to Martin Ganneker, who laid them ceremoniously onto the ice he had shoveled into boxes. You still could not see the sky and the fog drifted like smoke even into the shed where men drummed cards onto the barrel end, *bom, bom, bom.* Harper was almost dead for want of sleep, but he was confirmed now in his need for a boat. He felt the longing physically.

I wonder, he asked himself now, just when it was, what I was doing just that moment the rocket hit?

Martin never mentioned his son that night or all that morning. Well, Harper remembered, even though he was showing me plenty about the way his family had chased the bass, he never really said much out loud except do this or do that. And he never asked Harper out again, plainly preferring to work alone, even though Harper had done his share and had handled the fish pretty well, losing only one when the bass—maybe—wrestled down into a trench and dragged the line over a mussel bed. *Ping.* Harper thought he'd done remarkably well, for a kid. Maybe that's what scared old Martin off, Harper chuckled to himself. Maybe he figured a few more trips and one night he'd find me out there in the rips, loading up.

I'd have been a fool to try it, Harper thought. Those rips, in the dark, could tumble you. Crack your hull on the rocks out there and you'd be hard pressed to get any quick help. Yes, I was young and foolish, Harper thought, but not that foolish. I may have been a cocky little prick, but not that cocky. The water had killed his father, too, and he respected it. He wasn't so money hungry he had to go out in a gale. He could miss a day on the water now and then. He was getting to the age when he kind of liked a regular day off. Imagine telling his father that! Or old Ganneker, or any of the old-timers.

One morning after a really stinking day of lobstering, Harper rose especially early and put his goose gun in the car. He figured he'd had about enough. He didn't have any bullets, but he was going to put the gun where it would show and have a chat with Mr. Earl the Pearl Ganneker. At the fish house he picked up a barrel of cod heads for bait and learned from young Sammy Cash there that Ganneker had already gone out. First light was still an hour away.

"Did he buy much bait?" Harper asked.

"Not much," Sammy said. "He never buys much."

A little fog lay over the bay, but it was clearing and the gray water rolled in long, lazy swells. Harper figured if he put a little smoke on he might catch Ganneker off the Coast Guard Light where he sometimes made his first pull. There was still enough fog, though, that he had to throttle down. He didn't want to be chipping any paint off anybody's pride and joy.

Out at the Light, closer to open ocean, the water was pitching pretty good, and when he came through the fog bank Harper saw the *Dog Days* rocking and rolling just ahead in the dim light. He couldn't believe his eyes. Ganneker had two of Harper's floats right up on the transom! Harper put the shotgun on the console and motored up, slow. Ganneker only glanced at him, as if he could care less what Harper saw or thought.

"What the hell are you doing with my pots?" Harper demanded. He had to shout because the pitch of the water prevented him from getting too close.

"You're crowdin' me," Ganneker said. The gold tooth in his jaw sparkled. Ganneker's cheeks seemed hollow and his eyes lay deep in his head, ringed blue.

"I asked you a question."

"Fuck your question," Ganneker said. "And fuck your pots, too. Every damn day I've got to untangle these damn lines. Stop crowdin' me! You don't own this ocean."

"I'm not crowding you, you asshole," Harper cried. "You need more weight in your traps out here. Put another brick in those pots. The tide . . ." He broke off his explanation to back off a little since a swell had pitched the boat forward. "The tide out here, rips out. And for God's sake get more scope on your marker lines. When the tide comes up, your buoys are dragging your pots all the hell over the place."

"You're crowdin' me!" Ganneker threw the tangled, soggy, seaweeded lines down in disgust.

"I'm not crowding you, goddamnit!" Harper said. "Do it right and you won't have these problems." He swung away, leaving Ganneker to his tangles and his knots.

Do I believe that? Harper wondered. Do I believe he's pulling my pots to get the lines freed up? You'd think he'd notice how much weight I put in the traps, at least. He's got to be about as dumb as he is ugly, and by God he is ugly this morning. He looks sick. Harper spat over the side. Jesus! I come out here to raise hell and I end up teaching him to fish!

Harper decided to give Ganneker plenty of berth and headed off to Oyster Point. When he swung clear of the bar there and could see along the east shore a ways, he shouted in dismay. None of his markers—no, there was one, just one—was visible. He crawled in, leaning over the gunwale, stupefied and angry. The sun broached the horizon and for a moment the lingering fog lit up like neon gold. No storm last night, where the hell were his pots? Then he could see one, two markers just beneath the surface, the spires dimpling the water. He grabbed his boat hook and leaned out and down and hooked the lines, tugged them, but for Christ's sake, they tugged back!

Harper shook his head in disbelief, then put his back into the hauling. Some goddamn thing had tangled up in his pots and it had to be a pretty big goddamn thing because it had captured the whole line of them and the only big goddamn thing it could be, Harper thought, was a goddamn big-ass ghost gill net blown off, ripped off its stanchions until it wandered right in here and caught his pots, too! Harper hauled in fury, but it was a massive thing he had got hold of and he wasn't making much headway.

Mother said there'd be days like this, he told himself. He swore as he rested and then hauled away again until he caught the edge of the blue plastic net and confirmed his worst fear: goddamn ghost gill net. He wondered how much of it there was. Sometimes they reeled off miles of the stuff. Big enough anyway to snarl a dozen of his pots! And how long had it been drifting, catching and drifting?

Harper looped the plastic line over the end of the boat hook so he wouldn't lose it, and then one-handed in the cutty for a pair of cable cutters he normally used for chopping nylon rope. It was going to take all day, and it was going to wear him to a frazzle, but he couldn't see any other way he was going to save his pots than to cut the goddamn net apart bit by bit and foot by slimy foot, haul it out of there.

He had chopped and hauled through about a dozen feet of the net when he came across the first rotting bluefish. Harper snorted in disgust. Ten cents a pound, wholesale. I'll be lucky, he thought, if I don't find anything more unsavory than this.

About a month later, Harper returned to this same spot, only to find the *Dog Days* bobbing, swinging in the tide. The engine was not running, and as Harper crept forward he could not see Ganneker at all. The *Dog Days* lurched and spun and he approached cautiously. He expected to find Ganneker leaning over the gunwale and reefing on a stuck pot, but when he came around the boat's stern he saw Ganneker, or what was left of Ganneker, slumped against the console, a big red hole in his forehead and a splash of red above, the blood soaked all across his shoulders and a pool of it washing across the deck as the boat rolled. There was a pistol in Ganneker's lap.

"Jesus Christ, Ganneker!" Harper shouted. He came along-side, threw some fenders over, boat-hooked the *Dog Days* and looked at Ganneker and the blood and the gun until he believed what he saw. For a moment he thought of boarding and even taking the *Dog Days* out and pitching Ganneker into the sea, where he probably belonged. Harper thought about this for a moment, and then clicked on the radio and called the Coast Guard.

"Why don't you stay right there?" the dispatcher asked him.

"I got pots to pull," Harper said.

"Just don't let him drift too far. We want to make the pickup right away."

"I'll be here," Harper said.

"Don't get superstitious on me," the dispatcher said. "We appreciate it."

Harper remained fast to the *Dog Days*, but looked away and out to sea into the violet sunrise until the Coast Guard cruiser warbled in.

The news of Ganneker's suicide and Harper's discovery was all around Warrens Bay by the time Harper came in with his lobsters that afternoon. A small delegation of fishermen greeted him at the pier and for almost the first time in his life he had plenty of help unloading his catch. Everybody wanted to know the details, and Harper took his good time doling out the currency of what he knew. The delegation drifted over to Sandy's and after a few beers the speculation grew a little wild and Harper went home in disgust. Nobody seemed to get the essential thing, that he had seen something that would not let him sleep. After that, how in hell was he going to be able to close his eyes?

A few days later, when he came into the fish pier, he found Ray Stark awaiting him, glaring down from the pier, eyes bloodshot, his black beard quivering in the wind. Harper took

his time going about his business, unloading and cleaning the
boat, refueling, even though it was obvious Stark wanted to
talk to him and wasn't going to leave. Harper didn't know
what to say and he was a little afraid of Stark anyway. The last
rumor he'd heard was that Stark, when he got the news about
Ganneker, had flown into an incredible rage, thrown metal all
over his shop: the clanging and crashing of it went on for half
the night. Then he'd come out and hollered at the sky, and to
prevent himself from heading for the bars and sure mayhem,
he welded the bumper of his pickup right onto the side of the
building!

Harper dragged himself up the ladder and there was almost
not enough space between himself and Stark to step onto
the pier.

"I guess you want to know what I found," Harper said. "I
know you two were close."

"I guess I know what you found," Stark said. "That ain't why
I want to talk to you." He cocked his head. "I'm playing Santa
Claus."

Harper waited. "Don't play games, Ray. I don't know what
you think and I don't care much, really. But I didn't like what
I saw. It was some god-awful thing."

Stark turned and walked with Harper down the pier a ways
and then Stark just touched Harper lightly on the arm, indicat-
ing he should stop. From his rear pocket he pulled an envelope
and handed it over.

"What is this?"

Stark shrugged. "Read it. I give out about a dozen of these
today."

Harper tore open the envelope and found a note wrapped
around five one-hundred-dollar bills. The note read: *I took
your lobsters. About 100. This should cover it. Earl.*

Harper staggered a little. "What?"

"He had this box and a list," Stark said. "I just give these guys," he indicated the fish house, "letters, too. He's payin' them for gas he borrowed. And I got a few for the Fisherman's Supply and Sandy's and like that."

Harper stared down at the note, smudged with fingerprints.

"You want to buy a boat?" Stark said. "He give his boat and his pots to me. I'll give you a good price. I don't want 'em. I get sick just thinking about it."

"I'll let you know," Harper said. He shook his head. "Did you know he was planning this?"

Ray shrugged again. "No. But I ain't surprised. That was some pain he had. He'd lay there stiff as a board, eyes real tight, and he'd quiver. He made this noise, I called it his bee noise, but it wasn't funny to him. And sometimes he'd be scared. He'd say, 'Ray, I ain't hurtin', but I'm afraid I'm going to hurt.' Then we'd go drinkin'."

"You boys did some drinking," Harper said.

Ray started away. "You let me know about that gear," he said.

"Hey!" Harper called him back. "I'll pull his pots for you, all that I can find."

"Sell the lobsters, I don't care," Ray said. "Leave the pots out, use 'em. They're no good to me."

Harper folded the bills in half and stuffed them into the pocket of his pants. It wasn't all that many pots, he thought. But if he didn't use them, they'd just wander around out there, catching lobsters forever.